A Nugget of Time

Gold Club Series
Book 1

by
Mary Vine

A Nugget of Time
Gold Club Series Book 1

Contact Information:
authormaryvine@gmail.com
Melland Publishing, LLC
2017
Caldwell, ID 83607
ISBN-13:978-0-9966876-7-6 (paperback)
First paperback Edition: 2017
Editor: Lawrence Dean Carpenter

Table of Contents

Chapter 1

When Dixie Lea regained consciousness, she lay on her back and viewed the tops of evergreen trees spinning in the clouds. The last time she'd done this, she'd been a youngster spinning on one foot and flopping to the ground. Not a child now, she couldn't find joy in the moment, as a matter-of-fact, it downright terrified her. When the whirling stopped, she put a hand to her forehead and slowly made it to her feet.

Dixie searched her mind for the reason she stood in the middle of a forest. She took a deep breath of pine scented air and remembered walking into a hollowed out cave and stepping over a tiny stream of water that flowed down and out the entrance. Intrigued, she moved on, bit by bit as far as the sunlight streaked into the cave. Lightheadedness brought her to a halt and fearing a limited air supply, she pivoted to walk out of the tunnel. As she put out a hand to steady herself, she smelled the damp, musty walls. Near her fingers, spiders wiggled in the shadows giving her a loathsome shudder and in protection her shoulders went up and tightened to her neck. Despite the creepy creatures, her dizziness brought her to a standstill.

That was her last thought, standing in a cave, not in the middle of a forest. If she'd fainted, then how in the world had she landed out here in the thick of the woods? Could she have made it out here, to a side of a hill, on

1

her own power? She didn't think so, because as far as she could tell, she wasn't anywhere near the gravel road she drove in on.

Dixie had parked her car no more than two hundred feet from the cave, and waited for Ernie Welch to meet her at the entrance.

Ernie called the newspaper about doing an article on the largest gold nugget found since the early 1900s. She thought it strange he wanted to be interviewed out here, that he'd actually show her, a reporter, where he found the nugget; however, he did say he considered selling the property. She thought that was odd, too. Wouldn't he want to keep gold producing property? She definitely had questions to ask.

Now, with only the clothes on her back, she hadn't an idea how to find her car. "Okay, Dixie, what are you going to do?"

She'd left everything in the car while she went to check out the cave. She remembered just where she left her cell, in the middle of the passenger seat. *Not like she had reception up here, anyway,* she thought.

Hoping she was mistaken, she put her hands into the pockets of her jeans. Nope, she had nothing on her except jewelry. Dixie touched the diamonds nestled in her ears and then looked at her watch. It had stopped. She sighed while thinking it was only a month old and she'd certainly get her money back.

Momentarily the sun hid behind the clouds and she wished for a sweater. The weatherman promised a high of eighty degrees this morning, but that was in Boise and she now stood in the mountains of Northeast Oregon.

Perhaps someone didn't want her here; someone wanted the whereabouts of a gold producing site to remain a secret. So, maybe she did pass out and someone carried her away from the area. It made more sense than anything.

She wondered if she should stay put until whoever put her here came back. Yet, she didn't think it smart to wait around for someone convinced she'd tell others about the gold.

Twigs snapped in the distance and she held her breath. A moment later a deer moved into her line of vision and she relaxed considerably.

Okay, she'd leave. But which way should she go? She did an article on a survivalist that dispelled the myth that moss grew only on the north side of trees. True, the plant grew on the coldest or moist side, but it could also thrive on other sections depending on the overhead shading. He also said to stay where you are if you are a lost hiker so someone can find you. She shook her head and thought that if she could find a river or creek she could follow it to civilization. It made sense, she told herself, because people needed water to live. Bears and cougars needed water too, and wolves had returned to Northeast Oregon.

She had to stop scaring herself and be productive, keep moving until she could find water and decide where to go from there.

While marching through the rocks, grass, flora and trees of the forest, Dixie wondered how long it would take anyone to miss her. Janet at work would and she'd probably call her parents. Yet, she didn't want her parents to worry so she'd keep moving for as long as it took to find someone, or even better, a road to take her to her car. Also, with no shelter, food, clean water, or jacket, she'd be in need of rescue soon.

Her shoes weren't the sturdiest, but at least they were flats and she appreciated that.

Quickly, she became winded, not only from marching through the thicket, but from moving her arms to push away the unruly branches that scratched at her arms.

Later, about the time she lost all hope of ever finding civilization again, she heard voices. Booming male voices that made her halt instead of moving closer and calling for help.

Carefully peering between a tree and the branches of a bush, she spotted two men standing over a motionless man on the ground. They continued to bend over him and obviously no one wanted to administer CPR. Their smiles told her they were pleased he was either passed out or dead. Three horses stood grazing around them. One man leaned over and cleaned out the unconscious man's pockets, while the other searched a pack laying across one of the horses.

"I got it!" After showing the other what he'd found, they mounted their horses and one grabbed the reins of the third horse. Even though she could call out for help, she wasn't about to be rescued by murderers and thieves. Besides she was a witness to the crime.

In an instant she knew this had to do with the gold and the reason she was out here, and why this man had been struck down by two thieves.

Mentally, she made note of what they wore, hair color, facial features, age, and approximate height and weight.

Her fear of being found by these men was soon replaced by concern for this man lying on the ground. As soon as she could no longer hear the horses moving away, she scurried down an incline and across a well-worn path to the man.

Red blood pooled in the dirt and turned to black behind his head. His face froze into a scowl and his body, firm to the touch, told her rigor mortis started to set in.

"This is outrageous. How could someone actually do this?" With no answers, she turned and surveyed the area. They'd stolen everything but an old saddle bag. She wanted to throw up.

This poor man probably had family at home worrying about him. No doubt he'd been happy to find the gold that got him killed. Dixie tried not to look at the man any more than she had to, knowing this image would haunt her for the rest of her days.

She needed to call 911. With a sigh she decided right then and there she'd carry her cell phone in her back pocket from now on. A cell could probably work if she climbed up the mountain side.

Dixie took a few steps along the path and wondered what had made it. Anyone could see it was wider than a path made by deer or elk and she couldn't see any type of tire markings. Could it be along water?

After looking at the gap in the tree line, she walked closer. She pushed through the brush, and followed the sound of quiet, barely rippling water of a creek.

She wanted a drink, but wondered about the safety of the water. The water seemed clear enough, so she stuck her hand into the cool stream.

When James Brogan first saw her, he thought she was a man bending to take a drink. Within seconds he noticed tight breeches that exposed the small of her back, leaving no doubt that he was a she. He reacted immediately to the shapely woman, as females were far and few between in this territory.

"Good afternoon!"

The woman righted herself and turned quickly toward him. Her shirt, a style he had never seen before, fit snugly and came only to the belt line of the low riding breeches. He had never seen the likes of this costume anywhere in all his travels, and she looked too healthy to be a soiled dove. Further, he doubted prostitution could be her occupation as she looked from side to side, figuring a way to escape if need be. Still, she stood rooted to the spot.

"Hello," she returned. "Do you have a cell phone?"

"A what?"

"A cell phone," she said, louder this time.

He did not know what that was, but knew he did not have one. "No."

"I need to call 911."

"What?"

"I need to call the sheriff."

"There is not a sheriff in this territory yet, but I doubt he could hear you from here anyway."

Not only could the man not hear, but his sense of humor left something to be desired. Yet, he was handsome enough to make up for all his shortcomings.

He wore boots that went up to his knees, but different than any boots she'd seen, loose around the ankles, not fitted. His blue shirt looked to be made of a wool blend and the sleeves he rolled up exposed tan arms. His hat had a wide brim that sloped down in the back, whether by design or from wear she didn't know. An antique gun, belted low on his waist, looked like something she'd seen in a western.

"What are you doing out here?" he asked.

"I'm lost. Please follow me back to the trail, I want you to see something," she answered, speaking loudly so he could hear.

Dixie moved quickly to make space between them. He wasn't one of the men who'd killed the man, but with the gold in the area, she couldn't be too careful. No one could know she came to expose this rich area to the public.

Instead, James moved toward her, into her space. With an escaping breath of relief, she realized he cared more about the body on the ground. He bent and placed a hand on the dead man's shoulder.

"I heard a commotion so I headed this way," he said, not looking at her.

Apparently, with the traffic through here, the news about the gold had gotten out even without her newspaper article.

"He is dead," he said, more to himself than to her. "How did this happen?"

"I don't know," she said, clasping her hands in anguish after viewing the man again.

He reached forward and moved the man's chin enough to see the damage on the back of his head. He looked back at her. "Somebody hit him hard. What happened?" he asked slowly as if talking to an idiot.

"I don't know! I heard some voices...I was up there!"

His eyes scanned the area she'd pointed to and his eyebrows furrowed. "You do not need to yell, I can hear you." He waited for eye contact. "Do you know this man?"

"I don't know this man. Like I said, I was walking this way and I heard noise, too. I saw him, them, through the bushes."

"Standing from right through there?"

She nodded.

"A horse cannot get through there because of the thickness of the brush and trees."

"I'm on foot."

"Who was with you?" he asked with squinting eyes.

"No one." She moved a stray strand of hair behind an ear. When he continued to stare at her, she added, "I had an appointment to meet a man not far from here." She definitely would not mention the newspaper article. "While I was waiting for him, I stepped into a cave. I got dizzy and passed out, but when I came to I was lying on the ground not too far from here. I don't know what happened to me. Besides the scratches on my arms from the bushes, and a broken watch, I'm not harmed. Mr. A...what did you say your name was?"

"Brogan."

He didn't ask her name, only looked back at the dead man. When he turned, he asked, "Were you with him? Did he put those odd streaks in your hair and make you dress like that?"

After a second to comprehend, she said, "No! No, of course not. What's wrong with my clothes? And the highlights in my hair are called *auburn*."

He shook his head. "A lady does not walk around in the woods by herself, especially in an area filled with men and very few women. Some of the soiled doves around here are covered more than you are." After a moment, he added, "Did you hit him with a rock?"

This time she looked at him through squinting eyes. She'd like to hit *him* with a rock. "Listen, I don't know what a soiled dove is, but I don't like the sound of it. I did not come here with this man, but I'm nothing but concerned that an innocent man has been killed."

She stood taller. "I dressed myself this morning, thank you very much, and my *highlights* were done by one of the best hairdressers in Boise. Now, if you'd just point me in the direction of a cabin or house, I can call for help. Sheriff or no sheriff."

James decided this one was either crazy as a loon or had a lot of courage, but judging from her appearance, he fared to the side of loon. With chin up, she walked toward the path, in the direction he had come.

Dixie had nothing more to say to this man, besides she needed to get back to her car and leave this nightmare of a day.

True, there were crooks out here but she'd walk stealthily through the trees and bushes and listen carefully. She had to believe she'd be fine.

After taking a deep breath, she moved across the path the way she'd come.

"Where are you going?"

"I'm trying to get back to my car," she answered, turning slightly toward him.

"Do you mean the box*car* of a train?"

"Do you find it amusing to play games with words?" she asked, exasperated.

"I could ask the same of you. What car are you speaking of?"

"My car. My Toyota Camry. Good-bye." When she heard quick footsteps behind, she clenched and ducked her head.

"Relax, I am not going to hurt you, but you cannot travel out here alone. It is not safe."

She pulled her arm from his grip. "I'll be fine. Trust me."

"Did you hit your head? Is your head sore in any way?"

She ran her hands from her forehead to the back of her neck. "No. I passed out or fainted though. That I remember."

"Let me check your head."

"Why? I said I don't feel anything."

"Because some of the time you are not coherent."

Wasn't she? She thought she was, but then she did wake up to find herself on her back in the middle of a forest.

She turned around. "Search for yourself then."

"I hate to put my dirty hands in your clean hair." She could hear him brush his hands off along the legs of his pants.

"You have unusually soft hair. What kind of soap did you use to wash it?"

"Just the store's generic brand."

"I have not heard of that one."

"Yeah, well you've been in the woods too long."

"That I have," he said with a chuckle. He put his hands in her hair, but seemed to spend more time feeling the strands than searching for bumps. If she wasn't mistaken, he'd taken a whiff, too.

Her hair was silky all right, soft as a baby's, and smelled like nothing he had ever used. It must be this special soap, he decided. It was a scent that he could only compare to perfume.

For the second time, he wondered how she got these red stripes, intertwined in a uniform way, into her hair.

"Look for bumps, Brogan."

"I do not feel any bumps, and you did not experience any pain when I touched your head. The name is James."

Maintaining control of himself had been within his power for some time now. Mind over matter worked until he looked over her shoulder to the cleavage exposed at the v of her shirt.

The way she dressed, with her cropped short-sleeved shirt barely touching the waist of her tight fitting jeans, undid him. And if he, who could normally control himself, felt this way, how much more so the lonely gold miner or ruthless outlaw. Out here in this part, where few respectable women reside, a proper woman did not stand much of a chance alone.

Abruptly, his hands dropped to his sides and he hoped to keep them there.

Dixie stepped away thinking she certainly didn't need to stay and play touchy-feely, not with only so many daylight hours left to find her car.

"Well, we've decided I haven't hit my head and I feel fine, so good-bye James. Nice to have met you."

In a blink of an eye he grasped her, taking hold of the arm she'd used to wave him good-bye.

"What are you doing?" she asked, ticked.

"You cannot go alone."

She pulled her hand away and crossed her arms. "And why not? I came here alone."

"You are not safe out here."

"Because…"

"Women do not fare well in these mountains, except for fallen doves."

She shook her head. "What is a fallen dove, by-the-way?"

James stood silent for a moment and then blushed.

"Well?"

"Prostitute," he said quietly.

"Hey, wait a minute. You thought I was, am, a prostitute?"

He looked her up and down. "You do not dress like a lady."

"Geez," she said to the sky. "Where are you from?"

He frowned in return.

"Okay, not that I have time to waste here, but I can't resist. Describe how a lady should look."

"She should have her body covered."

Dixie pulled at her shirt. "This is in style. If you left the mountains for a few days you'd see what I mean. I suppose the next thing you are going to say is that a woman should only wear a dress."

"That is a common notion, yes."

"Well, I'll just take my immoral self and be on my way."

"I am telling you, you are not safe alone, but I am not going to hold you here against your will, ma'am."

James was a big man and could hold her here if he wanted to. Dixie surveyed the area around her. Could he be right? Were the thieves still out there? She believed it likely that they'd come back for more gold. If so, she'd be better off with him beside her.

"Why are you out here, James? Are you looking for gold, too?"

He nodded. "I am trying my hand at it, yes."

"I don't like not knowing where I am," she said.

"My guess is you are about three miles south of Cracker City."

"Okay. Cracker City."

"You will need a shirt or something to put on. I do not have an extra, but I can look in the dead man's saddle bag."

Dixie shook her head, but James missed it. She followed James back to the dead man. This time when she looked at him, she felt sorry for him. Gone before his time and it was wrong. *Wrong.*

"He does not have an extra shirt in here. What do you think about wearing his shirt?" he asked, pointing.

Besides the fact that the shirt looked to have been worn for weeks without washing, she couldn't find it in her to take the very shirt off his back, not when he'd been robbed of everything else.

"I can't take his shirt. It's not right."

"Then take mine." He was already unbuttoning his shirt.

"Are you sure?"

"Yes, ma'am." He handed his shirt to Dixie. "It is not too dirty."

It wasn't that clean either, rather dusty, but if it made him feel better she'd cover herself anyway. "Thank you."

Dixie buttoned the shirt and then looked at James. He had broad muscular shoulders that tapered down to a slim waist.

"You work out, I see."

"Out where?" he asked.

"You know what I'm talking about. A gym."

"I prefer to be called James."

The sad thing about it was that he didn't appear to be kidding. For that matter, he didn't smile much at all.

"I have worked outside and I have worked inside as well, if that answers your question."

The man didn't use contractions to shorten words in his speech. Perhaps it was that he didn't understand abstract conversation, and she wondered if he'd ever been hit on the head, or simply had a learning disability.

James tied the man's saddle bag, and the man, to the back of his horse. He laid him across the saddle as best he could as rigor mortis shaped him as he lay at time of death. It was disturbing to see anyone rigid like that, and a tear unexpectedly slid down her face. The man had certainly started today like any other, not knowing he'd die this day. Dixie hoped she'd be able to give enough information to the authorities to help them solve the case.

Chapter 2

Dixie turned her eyes away from the dead man to notice James's upper arms were nearly the size of her thighs. "Do you lift weights?" she asked, mimicking the movement with her arms and hands.

"I think I know what you mean. I have spent time helping out as a blacksmith, it is a very physical job."

A *blacksmith*? She didn't know there were blacksmiths around anymore.

She tried not to stare at James, but when he made the slightest move a muscle would ripple, so she gave up.

"You are staring at me."

"Sorry. Can't help it."

"Why are you staring at me?"

"You know the answer to that."

"I am not exactly sure. Tell me."

"Because you're hot, and I think you know that."

"Actually, I feel a cool breeze. I am not hot."

She watched his face. *He was serious!*

"Come *on*."

"I am moving ahead as fast as you are."

She couldn't help noticing that he raised an eyebrow. The man was slow on the uptake, that's all it could be, and she mentally told herself to not take advantage of a disabled man.

"Yes you are. Do you want your shirt back?"

"No. Cold or not, you cannot be seen as you are."

"Why is it that you can expose yourself and I can't expose the tiniest bit of skin? My shirt comes to my waistline, you know that."

He didn't answer, only gave her a perturbed look.

"I have to raise my arms for you to see any skin. I don't think you have anything to worry about. But you... Look, I can hardly keep my eyes off you."

"Have you never seen a man without a shirt?"

She chuckled; he made it easy to tease him. "I've seen very few, in person, that look like you," she said.

"In person, versus, not in person?"

"I'm referring to TV."

"TV? Do I dare ask what that is?"

There he goes again. Could he be kidding? Not that she could tell. "Never mind."

Dixie also wondered why he didn't comment any more about her staring. Was he that into himself? She shook her head; maybe she was too into *her*self. Well, if he didn't care she wouldn't worry about looking at him as much as she wanted.

James could not help but notice that Dixie continued to look at his chest. He believed she had a reason to do so. The way she dressed, the way she colored her hair, she was no lady. If he was right, she would verbalize it soon. She would want to entice him and get her pay.

Yet two things confused him. Besides how she adorned herself, her smooth skin and white teeth represented a very healthy woman, not a soiled dove. She appeared to be a woman of means enough to have a variety of foods, and she was far from looking worked to death.

Second, he was not so stupid that he missed the desire in her eyes, and he always thought prostitutes were in it for a whole different reason.

As they walked towards town, he wondered what to do with her.

"Do you have family near here?" he asked.

"No. My parents live two to three hours from here. By car."

"Yes, by car," he answered with a half-smile. "How did you get here, if your family is three hours away?"

Dixie wondered how much she should tell him. "I'm a newspaper reporter out of Boise and I was to meet a man out here about a story."

"Humph. I have never seen a woman working a printing press."

"Printing press? That's what you call it?"

He nodded.

"Well, you've met one now."

"When was the last time you worked?"

"Not counting this morning, yesterday," she said and sighed.

James caught himself grinding his teeth. Nothing about this woman made any sense. The more she talked, the crazier she became. "So you say you were at least three hours from here yesterday?"

"I was three hours away from you at eight o'clock this morning."

She sounded troubled. He would give her that.

"I need to find my car," she said, palms up.

She seemed so earnest that he had to give her the benefit of the doubt. "Describe this car."

"Thanks for not saying boxcar this time. It's a '15 Toyota Camry. White sedan, tan interior, four door. Twenty-eight miles per gallon."

"Perhaps you can draw it for me?"

"Sure. Have any paper? Something to write with?"

"When we get to town."

James did not know what a Toy-oat-a was, especially a four door one. *Her head was without blemish, so why is she confused about who, what, where, and how?* he wondered.

Dixie looked down, frowned and bit on her lower lip. "All right, tell me something about Cracker City."

"Has a main street that runs along a creek. It is a canyon, limiting the places to build. Wooden structures are being built along the canyon walls, as well, but you will see far more tents. I imagine with the presence of gold, more businesses will squeeze in."

James turned and put the back of his hand against her forehead, then touched his own.

"What was that for?"

"I was checking for a fever."

"And?"

"And you do not have one."

"I could have told you that."

"How do you feel?"

"Despite waking up in the middle of a forest, losing my car, and watching a murder happen, I'm just fine," she answered with a forced smile.

"Yes, I know you have had a hard day, but besides that, do you have a headache?"

"Physically, I feel fine considering I'm not in good enough shape for such a long walk. You could carry me, you know," she said.

His smile reached his blue eyes and they sparkled. A five o'clock shadow, now a few days old, grew ever apparent across his firm jaw and she noted a slight dimple in his chin. Her eyes moved up to his again and she noticed long dark lashes.

"Are you still staring at me?"

"Because you're a handsome man," she said, with a smile.

"You are a very forward woman."

"Just because I said you're handsome?"

"That is some of it, yes."

"I'm just appreciating what I see. You have fine shoulders, too."

He stopped and turned toward her and she noticed a red face.

"I've embarrassed you, haven't I?"

"I am not used to that kind of talk."

"Oh, come on. Surely you've heard it before."

"Ladies do not talk of a man's body in the presence of a single man."

So, he was single. "Yes, they do. You must have been hiding under a rock."

"I have been out of the city for a while, if that is what you mean, but not that long."

"Yes, you have a very fine body," she added to further torment him.

"What is it you want from me?" If he continued to stop and turn back, they'd never get anywhere.

"Ah, that is a good question. Right now I feel protected in your presence, because of your big broad shoulders." That was about it because attractiveness was not enough for her; she wanted a man with career goals, not someone who probably wanted to live off the land while searching for gold. Yet, she made judgments without really knowing him.

"How long have you been out here?" she asked.

"After the war I tired of the city."

When he didn't elaborate she said, "Did you return from service and go to the woods to find yourself again?" It would make sense after a stint in the Middle East.

"I am not lost. I came out here to find some gold before I decide to settle down."

"There are easier ways to make money."

"Like?"

"Going to school."

"I have been to school," he said and pressed his lips together.

He sure didn't want to elaborate. Yet, she didn't have anything else to do but talk, and she couldn't help but be curious about the man.

"Did you drop out of school to go into the service?"

"By service, do you mean the war?"

Interesting wording, she thought. "Yes."

"No," he answered bluntly.

"You don't seem to want to talk about the war."

"Not to a stranger, no."

She left it at that and they walked on in silence.

"I have to go to the bathroom. Do you have any toilet tissue in your pack?"

"Bathroom? Toilet tissue?"

Dixie let out a huge breath in frustration. "What do you use to wipe your behind?"

"Oh. Out in the woods I use hanging lichen."

"Hanging *lichen*?"

"Yes. Some is hanging on that tree over there," he said, pointing.

Dixie scanned James's face for any sign of humor, but came up lacking. She headed for the tree holding the *toilet paper*, while hoping that Cracker City wasn't too far in the distance.

***

A middle-aged man arrived in the city of Cracker, Oregon, during the morning hours. He'd walked a good distance and his legs were tired, so he sat down on the wooden walkway along Main Street and watched the townspeople pass by while he rested.

The gold-mining boom town had some men moving about the town, but most were panning for gold along the creek, or beyond in the rocky forest. Without the usual mining garb and tools he had to start as a common laborer in town and he came prepared to do most anything he could to earn his keep.

It took most of the day to walk into each business and proudly ask for work. No job, not even shoveling manure, could be found.

Traveling back down the boardwalk, he tried to remember the last time he had experienced such dismay and came up short. As he scanned the men around him, he felt the dismay turn to fear over where he would lay his head this night.

Chapter 3

Around a copse of pines, Dixie spotted a clearing. It was like walking into a living ghost town or a western, or a horror movie, she wasn't sure which. Scrappy tree stumps stood at the edges of the makeshift street, the tops removed to make more room, or to use as lumber. The dust blew in a breeze not strong enough to move the wood smoke out of the canyon.

She could see why a man's man would want to get away to a place like this, but on the other hand, she hoped it wasn't some dangerous sect of people.

Walking along Main Street they happened on a gathering of men outside what looked like a rustic bar. James took the gun from his waistband and held it so all could see as they walked by. The men leered at her like a band of construction workers and she ignored them the best she could. Dixie hoped they would take this antique of a firearm seriously. Although the only female, she wondered how she could take precedence over a dead man laying awkwardly over a horse.

Further down the street, they stopped at a barn where James opened the door and entered, horse and all.

"Stephen, do you know him?" James asked the man working with some sort of anvil. Glancing around, it amazed her that someone would work with this outdated equipment. As with the rest of this Podunk town,

Stephen was stuck in the 1800s. He put his tools down, gave her a once over and then looked at the dead man.

"I have seen him, yes. I think his name is Taylor. He has been talking about finding gold. Looks like someone believed him and took advantage."

Dixie perked up. *Could the finding of the massive gold nugget cause a town to form so quickly?* she wondered. If so, she had quite an article to write. Apparently, being the first reporter on the scene was a blessing.

Still, she didn't want to be here. She'd seen enough this day to make her long for civilization. Turning to Stephen, she asked, "Do you, or anyone around here, have a cell phone I can use?"

The man studied Taylor's head wound, but after a moment turned back and said, "I do not know what you mean."

Could it be possible that these men had been in the woods so long that they'd missed the rise of technology? More probable, the town only recognized the 1800s and took an oath to do so.

"Perhaps I should say telephone. Is there a telephone in town that I can use?"

His eyes narrowed in thought. "Nothing around here by that name, ma'am."

First James, and now this man pretending that he didn't know about phones. Pledge or no pledge, her heart picked up a beat realizing that no one wanted her to leave this place.

Not for the first time, James wondered what to do with this woman. Obviously, she was not safe here alone or anywhere within miles of here. He knew if he didn't lay claim to her, he would have to fight one or more to keep her safe. It was as simple as that. He had yet to see if she would agree to his plan, but it could not matter at this point.

"When is the stage coming through?" James asked Stephen.

Dixie smiled at what he'd said. They even had a stage coach with an actual route. Maybe she'd get a way out of here after all.

"Two days," said Stephen.

Her heart dropped with disappointment.

"I am sorry, Stephen. This is Dixie. She is my mail order bride."

Dixie chuckled at his humor, making her feel somewhat better. "Yes, tell him where I'm from."

"She is from Mesopotamia."

Dixie's jaw dropped.

Stephen rubbed his chin. "Where did you meet up with her?"

"Sumpter."

"You hitched yet?" Stephen asked, now giving her the once over.

"Yes," he said quickly.

Dixie had trouble closing her mouth. Were they all mad around here? Was she on some sort of secret camera show or a Twilight Zone sequel?

She felt gloom settle like a cloak around her shoulders. What could she do to get out of this place?

"Are there any other women here?" she asked Stephen.

"Sorry, ma'am, only soiled doves the other side of town. There is supposed to be a woman or two joining up with their men 'fore too long, though."

"Aren't there any women working in town?"

"No, Dixie," said James, with a look that told her to resign herself to the fact that he'd be in control of her for a while.

She couldn't give up just like that. She had to believe help was near; there were people here besides these two men. She'd hang onto hope. Deep in thought, she barely noticed James borrowing a shirt from Stephen.

Feeling paranoid, Dixie couldn't help but flinch at the gun James pointed at her feet, but after they cleared the barn, she understood why.

Men stood around the opening of the barn like dogs waiting for a bitch in heat. She scooted closer to James until they were hip to hip.

"What are you wearing?" asked one of the men making a half circle around her. They were dirty, unshaven, missing teeth and worst of all, stunk to high heaven.

"A…shirt and jeans."

"Jeans?" said another.

"What is your name?" asked another.

"Dixie is my wife. Let us pass through, boys."

"Dixie would be a southern name," said the one in front.

She wondered for only a second if she should ask one of these men for help. "No, I'm not from the south. Good-bye men."

They cleared the way, probably because James stood taller than any of them, but still they ogled her.

One of the men stopped at the walkway to watch the two until they were out of sight. He took a second look at the man and thought that the more than capable fellow would have been a friend he'd choose in his past. Now he had a woman, a beautiful woman, however, oddly dressed. A pang of envy hit him somewhere inside and he wondered at that for a moment.

How was it that a pretty woman was born with all it took to survive in a man's world? She would have a meal in her belly this night, provided by only a sweet smile, while he was no more than a scavenger, a pack rat looking for something shiny, in this godforsaken place.

Her luck made sure that she met up with this man, a big fellow with enough provisions to treat gold mining as a hobby he only dabbled at. This man could not only protect her, but provide until she tired of him.

The man's growling stomach moved his chain of thought to his unfair circumstances and anger flared within at this woman who made surviving look so easy.

Chapter 4

As they approached a cluster of tents, Dixie noticed they matched the antiquity of the rest of the town, probably made of some sort of canvas.

No spring-loaded, waterproof tents for these men. Similar to pup tents, they had one or two stakes to hold them up and a rope across the top made an A shape. *No wonder women didn't want to be here*, she thought.

"Do you have a tent?" she asked James and then held her breath as she waited for his answer.

"I have one, yes. Makes traveling easier."

Dixie didn't reply, just moved ahead wondering how many nights she'd be out in the elements before rescue.

One building caught her attention. She stopped in front of a newly built cabin with a window in front. If she wasn't mistaken a newspaper establishment took shape inside.

"I have to go in here, James." She didn't wait for his answer but he followed closely.

Two desks, without computers, caught her eye. On the top of one, outdated pens and ink bottles sat in front of a tablet. Two men turned her way, and for the first time she understood what printer's devils were; typesetters with rounded shoulders. One man was surely an apprentice or young assistant to the printer.

Advertising information was spread haphazardly across the other desktop and a glance at a nearby headline told her they were loyal to the Democratic Party. Even though the older man's body language communicated concern about her forwardness, she stepped to the rotary, iron printing press and studied the workings. The name Cottrel was embossed on the press.

"Does your paper say how much gold is found and by whom?" asked James.

"Absolutely," answered the young man.

"Can you really make a newspaper with this thing," she couldn't help but ask.

"A…yes, ma'am."

James took her by the arm and escorted her out the door. "That was rude. What are you trying to do?"

Dixie sighed. "To go back to this system, when technology has made things so much easier is ridiculous. In short order they'll see what I mean."

Even though excited about the stage and a way out of here, she couldn't help wondering about people who wanted to stay and pretend to live in another era. Certainly, she'd heard about people getting together, wearing an era's clothing, and pretending to be from that time. This had to be something similar. Whatever floats your boat, she thought.

He moved her along. "I am afraid to ask what you are talking about."

Not like he would admit to it anyway, she thought. "Humph. You didn't have to tell the men we're married. It'll put you in an awkward spot, when someone finds out differently."

"I did it for your safety. You are welcome."

"Humph."

"Stop saying that. Are you married?"

Dixie shook her head.

"A widow, then?"

"No."

"You are pretty and appear to be around twenty-five, so why are you not married?"

She stopped walking, crossed her arms and put a foot forward. "You're handsome and appear to be around thirty, so why aren't you married?"

"This is not about me, it is about you. I am not the one who is lost."

"Okay, okay," she said, sliding her arms back down to her sides. "I've been choosy, I guess. Especially since I can pay my own way."

James gave her what could only be called a placating smile and started walking again.

Thankfully, James had started to build a cabin and she didn't have to endure a makeshift tent in the cold of night. Dixie's father had a twelve by twelve storage shed in their back yard, and this structure was similar in size. The walls and roof stood erect, but the windows and doors were yet to be put in but she felt sure she could cuddle up in a corner and do all right through the night.

"You can sleep in here tonight and I can stay outside in a tent," he said.

"Don't be silly, I'll not move you out of your home. Besides, we're married. Did you forget so soon?"

He shook his head. "I do not want you to feel uncomfortable."

"I won't be." It touched her that he cared about her comfort. He'd shown that he was a gentleman in many ways.

"I will not touch you, so you need not worry."

"I won't touch you, either," she said with a smile and his eyebrows nearly touched his hairline.

"How do you keep your horse from running off?" she asked, changing the subject so he wouldn't choke. "Is he trained that well?"

"He minds, but he can get spooked, so I tie him to a horse tether."

"Tether did you say? I don't know what that is."

"Come to the window. Now look on the ground in front of him. That circle of iron weighs fifty pounds and he will not drag it far. At night I tie him to the house."

"Wow. I've never seen one of those before."

"I suppose in Mesopotamia they do not use these," he said with a smile, but then his eyebrows came together as if he had concerns about her.

Who had not seen a horse tether? James wondered. Not so long ago he wondered if Dixie had hit her head in an accident, but now he only questioned her honesty.

"Oh, yes, Mesopotamia. Why in the world did you say I was from there?" she asked.

"Because of the way you are dressed. Not much is known about the way a woman dresses in Mesopotamia, I am thinking."

"Okay," she said, the word drawn out and then she puckered her lips to the side for a moment.

"We can get a dress for you tomorrow. I saw some in the general store."

"Is there a money machine in town?" she asked, then shook her head. "I don't have a card, but even if I did a money machine wouldn't match the scenery around here."

She appeared to believe every word that came out of her mouth, and he found it disconcerting. If this was crazy, then it was a creative crazy, being able to make up words that had nothing to do with the modern day. The truth would come out eventually, as no one could keep this up forever.

"Since you're building a cabin, looks like you plan to stay here awhile."

"Yes, for now. I will look for gold, and when I tire of that, I will sell and move on."

"To where?"

"I am not certain." A stranger did not need to know his plans.

Dixie walked to the other window and looked out. "I'll have to pull up my dress to keep it from dragging in the dirt, you know."

It was hard for him to believe a woman did not want a new dress. "We will see what they have at the store, Dixie."

"Huh. You're using square-headed nails. I didn't think anyone made them anymore. Now that's dedication."

"Yes." James could not play her game at the moment due to hunger and exhaustion from trying to figure out what to do with her. "Let us eat."

Dixie smiled again at his lack of contractions in everyday speech, as if using them ranked low on his standards of proper English. She watched him move about the cabin and wondered how much cooking he could manage without a stove or microwave. Still, from his things he produced a hunk of bread, some wine, cheese, and some sort of jerky. She didn't realize the extent of her hunger until she took a bite. The tasty jerky had to be homemade. The packaged stuff at the grocery store seemed like synthetic leather compared to this. James took his knife and skimmed an edge of white mold from the cheese. The cheese and bread tasted homemade as well.

"I have ordered a stove. It will help me cook and keep me warm."

"You must mean a wood burning stove."

"Of course, yes."

He picked up a board and went to the window nearest her. In an effort to help, she stood and lifted a side of the board and started to hammer in a few nails.

"This is temporary of course. The board will help keep the heat in tonight," he said.

"And the men from looking in the window," she added.

He nodded.

"You'd think they'd have something better to do with their time. Wait, no internet. Maybe not."

He silently finished the job.

"Thanks for helping me, James. You're a good man."

"Nothing more than any Christian would do."

***

Dixie wrapped herself up in a wool blanket and waited for blessed sleep, but it was hard in coming. James tossed and turned so she knew he had the same problem.

"Where did you grow up?" she asked.

"Oregon City. My father works for the Hudson Bay Company as a chief trader."

"A chief trader. Is that like a trader for a hedge fund?"

"What? Hedges? Oh, you must mean the fire-managed prairies and plains. He is part of that as well."

"I mean like a consultant."

"Yes, he does that, too."

Not much complexity in his thinking, she realized again, and she didn't have the energy to try and help him understand the two meanings of the word hedge. "Huh. Interesting career."

"I suppose."

If she could catch him referring to the actual century they lived in, she would so enjoy it. "So, where did you go to college?"

"Willamette College."

"I guess you didn't want to go into your father's business."

"No, present times have changed the business. I studied law. You ask too many questions."

"I want to say one more thing."

"All right, one more thing," he said with a sigh.

This statement could get him to tell the truth, if nothing else would. "I studied the Civil War in school, and I want to say that I'm thankful for your service and am so sorry you had to endure such a terrible war."

"That is one of the nicest things anyone has said to me," he said quietly. No one had ever stated it like that before, and he felt proud.

"Really? Well, I'm glad I said it, then. Were you injured?" She said the additional question quickly so he wouldn't notice. He smiled.

"A sword stabbed into the flesh of my thigh. I am blessed to recover from such a wound."

Ah ha! she thought. *Got him.* "I will look at your wound tomorrow."

"You will not look at my body."

"I said I wouldn't touch it. I just want to look at it."

"It's not appropriate for a lady to look at the thigh of a man."

She had him now. "Better yet, light the lamp again and I'll look right now. Then we can go to sleep."

"I will not sleep after you look at my thigh. I am a healthy male."

"Oh, you're pathetic. I'm going to light the lamp."

She pulled and twisted out of the blanket and crawled to the lamp. "Help me here. I don't know how to light this."

"You have never lighted a lamp? Now who is pathetic?"

"Not like this. Come on."

He pulled the cover to his chin. "Perhaps you have some medical training. Is that it?"

"Nope. Come on, you baby."

Obviously she made him mad enough to reach for the lamp. In seconds it lit, and he pulled his pants to his knees and wrapped the blanket around the bottom of his torso.

"You said you were not going to touch me."

She pulled back her hand. "You are more modest than any man I've ever known."

"You mean you have done this before?"

"Relax, James." She moved the lantern closer. "Dang, you have a scar."

"A stab wound produces a scar, Dixie."

It was a nasty one, like he didn't have it stitched up correctly, at least according to today's standards. It left an indentation on one side and a lump on the other. The opening was the size of a sword, she'd give him that.

She put the lamp down and he blew it out. After he'd put his pants back on, she asked, "Tell me what really happened, I won't tell anyone."

After a few moments of silence, he said, "We were in the woods and could not see the enemy coming." The timbre of his voice made him sound like it was hard to squeeze out the terrible words. "The Rebs nearly took us over. Many died beside me. Friends, by then - "

"You should be in Hollywood," she cut in, then turned over, ready to sleep.

Dixie said Hollywood in a rather sarcastic manner. James did not ask about Hollywood, a place he had never heard of, for two reasons. He wanted to believe her sane and did not want hurt feelings. However briefly, this was the first time he had shared the war with anyone. Something about her made him want to open up and speak, and he wondered how she managed it. He liked that she had no guard with him, that she spoke her mind even as a woman. The woman had spunk, he would give her that.

Yes, most of the time he liked to watch the words come out of Dixie's full lips, and the way her hips swayed as she walked, with the small of her back highlighted by tight jeans. Sadly he had grown used to the concealing of the female form by a dress. So, obviously, his heart picked up a beat when she asked him to take off his pants, and still he did not know why she wanted to see his scar. He had always feared a woman would swoon at an injury like this, a scar to be hid in the dark. This was not the case with Dixie, a curious woman for sure.

James wanted to wake Dixie up, spend as many moments with her as he could, since she would be gone on the next stage. Instead, he listened to the even breathing of sleep. If he could, he had tomorrow and the next day to figure her out. He tightened the blanket around him and stared into the darkness for some time before dozing off.

***

The miner arrived in this town with only a pocket knife, wallet with nothing useful in it, keys that no longer unlocked his spacious home and a measure of fear. The first time he saw miners at work, he looked for anything he could dig with, a broken tool, sharp stick, or a small handful of square-headed nails. With a small streak of luck he found a tin can he used to pan for gold.

To get the proper language down and learn about life and mining, he listened to men in the mining camps. At night, he waited until everyone turned in, and then searched for anything around the tents to help him survive. On a good night, he'd also find a newspaper, or parts thereof, to keep up on the headlines.

Perhaps the lowest of the low, he picked up cigarette stubs to smoke in the shadow of the night while he contemplated what he'd done in his life to deserve such a fate.

While trying to steady his thoughts and hold on to the thimble of hope he had left, he moved on to the forest and his pile of fir limbs for a partial night's sleep.

Chapter 5

Dixie woke up with a smile, until she remembered being caught in a time warp. She turned over to see the best part of this nightmare across the room. To confirm it, James gave her a gorgeous ear-to-ear smile, and she wondered what he was so happy about. The poor guy was stuck with her until he put her on the stage.

The stage wouldn't be her best bet, she suddenly realized. Someone could have her purse, identity and credit cards, long before the stage arrived. Also, if she couldn't check in at work her boss would be upset. She visualized him staring at his cell waiting for word about the much anticipated gold article. She liked her job in Boise and intended to keep it.

"James?"

"Good morning."

"Yes, good morning. What are your plans today?"

"I plan to work on the cabin until the stage comes along. Something I need to do anyway."

Dixie could ask about a shower, but he'd only say, "What's a shower?" The meaning of bath or bathe, he'd admit to knowing, but her fresh mind suddenly reeled off onto another possibility. This new plan didn't require a shower until she made it back to her own home.

She sat up and rubbed her face. "I know where the gold is."

"Of course you do," he replied, his tone placating. He was good at that.

"I didn't fully explain what brought me to the area."

"Oh?" He sat down at the edge of her blanket, now clearly interested. *Good sign*, she thought.

"My boss, at the newspaper, told me that he'd heard of a man who'd found a huge gold nugget and he wanted me to write an article about it. I talked to the gentleman who owned the property, and he told me to meet him at the mine."

"If you already talked to him, then why do you need to go to the site?" he asked.

Good question, she thought. *No cell phones in 1800s.* "He wanted me to see the property. A few minutes after I arrived at the mine, while waiting for the owner, I walked into a cave. I fainted, then lost my way and eventually found you."

His eyebrows furrowed. "Why did you not tell me this before?"

"I was afraid I'd be in danger if I told anyone about the mine. I thought that Taylor died because of it."

"But now?"

"I don't have any money, so I need to find some gold."

James stood up, folded his blanket and then reached for hers. She pulled it from under her and handed it to him.

"And where is this site?"

At least he didn't say no. "Can you find the way back to where you found me?"

"Yes."

"I'm thinking it's about forty minutes on foot from that point. As you know, I didn't have any kind of tools with me at the time."

His eyes narrowed. "What do you know about this man?"

"He was about fifteen minutes late when I fainted. I'm thinking he changed his mind about showing me where he found the gold, and carried me away from the cave. That's all I can think of."

Dixie wanted out of town, but did not verbally express it. Not saying so was unusual for a blunt woman such as herself. Who could blame her for wanting to get out of a dirty man-filled town without a decent woman to befriend?

She did say she wanted to keep her job as a writer and pay her bills, as any man would want. Yet, most women did not talk this way to anyone but family. Dixie did not have the arms or back of a gold miner. The hard work required a certain mindset, which she probably had, but her strength would betray her.

In a dream scenario, James wanted her to say that she would stay by his side no matter where they went. He understood feelings could be one-sided, probably a good thing as this woman only just now told the truth.

"We will go today. After a visit to the store."

Dixie squealed in delight and jumped up to hug him. He held her a little longer than he should have before turning to gather the day's food.

"Don't forget your antique weapon over there," she said.

"My what?"

She chuckled, then waved her hand like never mind. "You so fit into this world."

He took that to mean she did not.

***

One thing she'd never get used to was the hanging lichen. If nothing else could make her leave Cracker, toileting procedures would. The only thing she enjoyed about Cracker was handsome James and the forest around him. A prettier area and a better man she'd have a hard time finding.

After attaching his saddle and bag to the horse, James loaded a pick, shovel and pan. It amazed her how he could fit so much in such a little space.

He stood behind, hefting her over the horse.

The silence between them seemed to last forever, until Dixie said, "Will you come and see me in Boise?"

"Where?"

"Boise, Idaho," she answered, drawing out the word Idaho.

"I am aware that Idaho became a state, if that is what you mean by your tone of voice." After a moment, he added, "You must mean the area over by Idaho City."

In this stupid world he adhered to, Idaho City, an old mining town, must have developed before Boise. "What year is it?"

"That is an odd question. You know it is 1870."

"Of course I do. Just seeing if you knew."

"Humph," he murmured.

He was so good at this game. Before long she'd be good at it, too. *Heaven forbid.* "Okay. From here, on the best road, you come to the Boise area first."

"Why do you want me to come to *Fort* Boise?"

Oh, for Pete's sake. Instead of rolling her eyes, she took a deep breath and refocused. "I've come to think a lot of you, is all."

"You have?" he asked, smiling.

"Certainly. You're a good man and would make a good friend."

"Thank you," he answered but lost the smile. "Being a good person is expected of us all."

"Yes, it is what we're taught from an early age, but somehow people forget that and replace goodness with greed, ambition, or selfishness."

"The meek will inherit the earth," he replied.

"Not this earth, but in heaven, I'm thinking. People, me included, are so tired of crooked politicians."

"Yes." He stopped and turned toward her. "Did you study law as well?"

"No, you'd just have to be blind not to see it."

"I disagree; many have faith in their leaders. But I did see the things you speak of, enough to make me want to take a break from law."

Of course, he meant 1870. "People will see it eventually. Wait, you're a lawyer?"

"I studied law. It is obvious." He frowned, then picked up his pace and the horse he pulled made an effort to keep up.

"Do you want to talk about it?" she asked, noticing shift of mood.

"No."

Dixie slid off the horse on Main Street. James started to open the door for her, but she reached for the handle first. After tugging on the large door, she stepped aside. "Why do they have to make such a tall door? Are they expecting giants?"

He chuckled in response.

The scent of leather reached her as she searched through the old fashioned general store. Not seeing anything that caught her interest, she said, "The clothes on my back are fine for now, but boots for the walk would certainly be helpful."

She stopped in front of the small shoe section. "Where's the hiking boots?"

"These boots work for all the walking and working we need to do," he answered in a low, but firm voice.

"A...okay." It wasn't her penny anyway. "The prices are so low, I don't see how the owner can make a profit."

"I thought the exact opposite. He is charging more for convenience."

"You guys are so funny," she answered with a chuckle.

Yet his eyebrows slanted up, apparently not understanding her humor, but she wasn't as used to the dedication of these people to all things 1870.

Amongst a smaller man's shoe size, she found a fit. Afterwards, she stood and surveyed the rest of the small store. Compared to what she was used to, most of the clothes had to be domestic, as well as simple kitchen utensils and tools. She picked up a pair of women's underwear and waved it in the air. "He must be expecting Grandma to arrive soon."

James's face reddened, so she shrugged her shoulders and put them down.

The dresses were out of the question, but she found a long skirt that could work with the boots, and a floral blouse that might bring out the blue in her eyes.

"What no plus sizes? Women were thinner in your time-line, I suppose. But, you can bet some female will get upset about the unfairness of it all."

James didn't answer and his gaze shot to the shopkeeper, probably to see if he stood within ear shot. Most likely there was some kind of punishment for not sticking to the era. *Rather creepy*, she thought.

"James, I'll come back and get the skirt and blouse if it takes me awhile to leave town."

"We will get them anyway," James replied while grabbing a set of Grandma's underwear and socks.

"I'm not wearing that tight thing around my waist, if you're thinking of buying that corset thingy as well," she said, jabbing her finger in the air. "My waist is just fine and you know it."

James pulled his hand back before touching the garment, embarrassed because he knew the shopkeeper could hear her words.

At the counter, the clerk tried to add up the total while ogling her jeans under the long shirt he had loaned her.

"I'm his mail order bride from Mesopotamia," she told him. "We know how to dress over there."

The man frowned, apparently not understanding, but said, "I figured you was married."

Dixie motioned with her hands as if the man dense or hearing impaired. "Do you have a trinket to pull my hair back with?"

"Oh, yes," he answered and set some kind of clip down on the counter.

James grabbed a tablet and a couple of pencils.

On the boardwalk, he said, "As we did before, we will take turns riding the horse. I am freshest in the morning and can walk for miles so that will be good for you."

"Why not ask me when I'm freshest?" asked Dixie.

"No need to ask, I can tell by looking at you."

Her brow wrinkled. "Oh yeah? I have pretty good muscle tone. I'm a runner."

He could not help but smile. "And where do you run to?"

"Don't be a dork. I run three miles, three times a week."

"I do not know what a dork is, but I do not like the sound of the word. And again, where do you run to or from?"

She sighed so hard the horse glanced back. "I have never had such a difficult time having a conversation with anyone."

"I would have to say the same," he answered, taken aback by her tone of voice.

"Okay, I'll play along. It might just make the time go faster. In Mesopotamia, people have realized that a body in motion is a healthier body, so we decided that we should exercise to make our bodies stronger. Sitting is as bad as smoking, we now believe."

"I have long believed smoking to be bad for the lungs. But, why not just work hard instead?"

"Because," she said as if talking to a child, "Some jobs are stationary. Many have to sit at their desks all day, or stand in one place."

"Sounds like a boring job to me. Even so, there is wood to cut and gardens to tend to. Cooking and cleaning and washing clothes at the river."

"Okay, you win. In 1870, I wouldn't need to run."

"You did not answer me about this running you do."

"And I'm not going to either."

They passed by several gawking miners on foot, donkey, mule or horseback. James turned to her and said, "The staring is different. They have heard we are married, I am thinking."

"Good, I guess."

He nodded, firmly.

"This is a nice horse. I like the curve of his neck, very regal. What kind is it?"

"A Morgan horse."

"Tell me about the Morgan horse."

"You have not heard of a Morgan horse?" He couldn't believe she had not heard of a widely used horse. More of her games, he knew. "The Morgan horse was created by a man named Justin Morgan. It is a compact, but strong horse with good temperament. Good for pulling wagons. Both the North and the South used the breed during the war. Miners use them, too."

"In all seriousness, that's a nice piece of history."

"I guess you could say that, yes."

Dixie supposed it could be fun trying to keep in line with the times, a fun sort of challenge to a lover of the era, but James didn't appear to enjoy having to work at keeping his world back in 1870. Instead, he acted like the things of the present confused him, in the vein of not understanding in the first place. He didn't appear to kick into mode when she talked in the present, only caught off guard by her comments. Clueless would be the word she'd choose. Yet, he didn't appear to be an intellectually challenged man by any means. If she continued to talk of the present, the lines across his forehead would be deeply engraved.

Further, she believed his concern had nothing to do with fear of being caught by any group. She wanted to ask but didn't want to offend him with more questions about the subject.

"Have you ever been thrown by a horse?" Dixie asked.

"Yes, but do not worry about this boy. He is trustworthy."

"Did you get injured in the fall?"

"No, that was a long time ago, as a teenager learning to ride a challenging horse."

"How about you?" he asked, looking her squarely in the eye, at least between steps.

"I haven't ridden a horse in many years. I remember a friend's horse tried to knock me off by taking me under a tree limb."

"Yes, an untrained horse will do that. Did you hurt yourself?"

"No. But not even in the war?" she shot in.

He was quiet for a few minutes, looking like he had to force himself back to a hellish time. Finally he said, "Nothing that really hurt me, no."

A fear sliced over her, making her think she really was in 1870, until she mentally chastised herself for it. She'd feel so much better behind the wheel of her car.

"I thank you for helping me, James."

He smiled, coming out of his funk. Such a serious man, she wished he'd smile more often.

"My dad always said that the forest was like going to church for him, that God was ever present here," Dixie said, taking in an extra breath of the sweet air.

"I can see how he would say that. In times of peace and stillness, I can feel Him. Probably one of the reasons I came here, to take stock of my life; to move away from the past and seek direction for the future. But, war entered the forest." After a moment he said, "I would like to remind you that as a woman you should always beware out here, and not travel alone. You need to have more of a fear of it, I am observing."

She tried to shift him to brighter thoughts. "I look forward to a day when families can safely come here to camp and enjoy the environment."

"That is a good notion, Dixie."

Chapter 6

The miner stood behind a pine and watched Brogan and Dixie go by. As a matter-of-fact he'd been sneaking along watching them since they left their cabin. No one noticed him because all eyes were on Dixie, now the jewel of the town.

Dixie would never spot him as the wench kept her chin up and eyes away from others, pretending to focus all of her attention on Brogan. He believed his first name should be Fool, as she started to lead him down a literal and figurative path out of town. She'd get him killed most likely.

Something dark inside him twisted and turned as he looked at Dixie. Certainly, the tables would turn on her good fortune one day. One day soon, he'd wager.

***

James didn't take a turn on the horse, instead acted like he could walk forever. When they finally stopped, he put his hands around her waist to help her down, and she took advantage by hugging him fiercely on the way down. When her feet touched the ground she kissed him on the cheek.

"You ought not to touch me like that. It is not ladylike."

"Maybe I like you and want to touch you."

He liked her too, but touching was not the wisest thing to do. Yet, in a second's time, she pulled him to her again.

"Loosen up, big fella. It's all right."

His mouth was open in surprise when she kissed him full on the mouth. Her tongue lightly fanned his bottom lip before she stepped away. "Nice lips," she said.

This was no peck on the lips but the kiss of a lover. "Please, Dixie. You do not have to do that. I will not take advantage of you in return for help."

She chuckled. "I know that. You're a gentleman, and I thank you for your good care."

He shook his head. "Remember, I am no different than any other Christian man who would help a woman in need."

"A damsel in distress?"

"I suppose. Yes."

After laughing out loud she said, "I hope no one takes advantage of your good heart."

"No one does," he said, his jaw firmly squared. "You might be the first one."

Her face went through several motions while she considered his words, followed by a moment of silence that troubled him.

"I'm attracted to you, which may or may not be news to you," she said.

"What do you mean by attracted?"

Dixie gave him a melancholy smile. "I find you sexy. You know, physically attractive. I want to put my hands on you, but I'm sorry you don't feel the same about me. I'd hate it if someone did that to me. I guess I finally realize my forwardness, as you might call it, is repulsive to you. I've thought too highly of myself. I'm sorry to put you in a situation that you don't like."

James kept his eyes to the ground so she could not read his face. This was the perfect time to confirm her words and keep her at a distance as it should be. But hearing her terminology, plus a kiss that made him speculate, was something a red-blooded man such as himself could not let go.

He dared a quick peek at her face. He could not leave her in such a pitiful condition, thinking herself unworthy. Yet putting her down a measure might be the best thing.

"Why aren't you saying anything?" she asked, chin up. "Are you trying to find the right words for this delicate topic?"

The girl had courage, which made her even more attractive in his eyes. He chortled in what came out as a forced sound, until he cleared his throat and started laughing. Harder and harder he laughed, until he had to sit down on a boulder.

"I'd laugh with you if I understood the joke." Her delectable lips moved into a straight line.

Leaning forward, he laughed again, eyes closed, not seeing her approach.

"For a guy who never smiles, let alone laugh, this must be a very humorous issue to you." Her arms were crossed, probably keeping her from slapping his face.

With great willpower, he calmed himself while letting out short sighs and moans that made her eyes widen. What could he say now, but the truth?

He rubbed his face with both hands. "Oh, I have not laughed like that since before the war."

Her eyes narrowed. "I'm glad to hear that, but at my expense? What happened to Mr. Nice Guy?"

Color had touched her already beautiful cheeks. He put his hands to his mouth to keep from laughing again. "Sorry," he said in a slurred voice.

"That's all you're going to say, after I lowered myself before you?"

In response, he leaned back with laughter. "Ahhh. Stop talking for a moment. Let me settle down."

"Want me to slap it out of you?"

"No, no. Give me a moment. Ahhh. You sure make life interesting, do you know that?"

"Interesting?"

Obviously, she found the word offensive.

Dixie grabbed his wrists and held them in the air as best she could. He needed to sober, so she could forget this stupid conversation and move on to finding her car.

"I meant interesting in a good way."

"Well, thanks. I guess," she said with a sigh. "Since you don't like my hair, or my clothes, or my kisses, interesting will have to do."

Dixie wasn't shallow; physical attractiveness wasn't all she'd hoped to attain in this life. Her parents helped her learn how to nurture a good self-esteem by raising a good student, a hard worker, to know what her strengths were and how to use them. She had every confidence in herself as a human being. "Now let's go."

"Wait, you must not think so poorly of yourself. I am getting used to your hair; it shines beautifully in the sun-"

"Thank you one more time," she interrupted.

James shook his head repeatedly. "That did not come out right."

"It sure didn't."

He stood and she stepped back. "I think you are beautiful, and a very attractive-"

"But not to you, you've made that clear, James."

"To me. Yes, to me," he said in his nice guy tone of voice, his face changing back to the James she knew.

"I hope you are not placating me," she warned, tapping her foot, even though she wanted that happy man back. "Gosh, we're sounding like an old married couple."

She knew he wanted to smile, but she shot him a warning glance.

"No. I am not placating you. I find you attractive and sexy."

"But not sexy to you."

"You are sexy to me."

For goodness sake, he blushed.

"Loosen up, James."

His scowl told her he was dead serious.

"I take offense that you thought I was making my way by trying to give you…favors."

"What kind of favors? See, I am loosening up, as you call it." Yes, there was a crack in his shield.

"That's not me. I just want you to know that. Next time, I'll wait for you to kiss me."

She couldn't help but flirt, yet turned away so she couldn't see his face, not wanting to see the returning concern he wore like a mask. In truth, she longed to see him laugh and be happy, and to have more than a glimpse of the man he once was.

***

Dixie made it to where they'd originally found the dead man. By now she should be observing yellow police tape and a law enforcement crew checking out Taylor's murder scene. Apparently the *town* planned on keeping the man's death a secret.

"You can get on the horse," she said, turning back toward James. "I want to walk the way I came in. It should be about forty-five minutes to meet up with you the first time we met."

"I imagine at your pace the horse can sleep while walking. Maybe you should run?"

She started walking, but turned to smile at his humor. "Humph. These boots are not easy to run in."

"As I told you when we met it is hard to get a horse through these bushes."

"I was on foot, remember?"

James raised his leg over the horse and slid to the ground. "I will walk him up the hillside."

To keep herself from worrying about someone stealing her car, she focused on marching her new boots up the hill. Branches and bushes impeded her journey and she wondered why she didn't stress over spiders the first time around.

Regardless of an active lifestyle, Dixie's whole body struggled upward, while James didn't even appear winded. When they came to a clearing, he offered her the horse, but she shook her head. He effortlessly climbed onto the Morgan.

"What's his name?"

"He does not have a name."

"I'll think of a good one," she said, happy with the duty.

"No, naming a horse makes you too close to the animal."

Just before she opened her mouth to say something contrary, he held a finger to his lips.

Hearing footfalls before she did, James had a hand on the handle of his gun. A man stepped slowly into the clearing and let out a breath of relief when he spotted James.

"Good day, Lieutenant Colonel," he said and saluted. When James only nodded, he went on his way.

"Wow. A lieutenant colonel," she said in amazement. James frowned while watching the man travel out of his line of vision.

Unsure of how this community worked, and since he hadn't responded, she asked, "Did you choose to be a lieutenant? Or should I say, can you choose to be a lieutenant colonel?"

"I will answer your question by saying, if I felt I had a choice, I would not have entered the war."

If she could look up the word taciturn in the dictionary she'd find his picture.

Dixie scanned the area in front of her and they moved on along a path made by animals.

His expression turned from taciturn to sullen.

"I'll soon be out of here and you can go about your life, if that's what you're worried about."

"What? No, I am not worried about that."

James was not worried because he knew she would not find this car she talked about.

"So, it's not me that's making you frown so?" she asked, squinting.

"No, you do not make me frown...usually."

She stopped walking, which was a good thing since her eyes weren't on the path before her. "Oh."

"Oh, what?"

"You have PTSD."

Maybe she did worry him. The way Dixie said the statement made him think the acronym stood for a bodily disorder, and she felt sorry for him. "Whatever that is, I can assure you I do not have it."

Her face told him she doubted his confession. "Tell me what the initials stand for."

"Post-Traumatic Stress Disorder." She searched his face for a moment and then turned away, abruptly closing the subject.

He did note that she did a better job at controlling her outlandish comments, letting them drop as she did now. Perhaps in reflection she knew she could not fool him.

"I have paper and a pencil, you know."

"Yes, I saw you buy them."

"Stop a minute." He jumped down and reached in his pack for the items. "I want you to draw me a picture of your car."

"Oh, for Pete's sake! Come on."

"Why are you having a problem with this? Can you not draw?"

Dixie could draw and pretty well, but she wasn't going to waste time and energy trying to convince this rule follower of a man that he lived in any year past 1870. Yet, he seemed so serious, not accusing in any way. "Do you doubt me?"

"You seem so sure of this car and I want to give you the benefit of the doubt. Perhaps it is something I have seen somewhere."

"Not in this community." After a moment, she said, "Let's go, I'd rather show you in person."

"If that is what you wish, then."

"It is. Tell me about your time in the big city. I know you practiced law. And tell me about society."

"People were happy to have their men folk home from the war. For those that were not so fortunate, they struggled to put their lives back together. Those of us who did return, felt guilty at times, that good men were taken whilst we remained."

"You must have been so thankful to be alive."

"Not always."

She couldn't imagine James being suicidal. "I hope keeping busy helped."

"It did, but I had seen men at their best and worst and the true nature of man, while the problems of the town's men seemed small and petty. Ignorance, anger and greed exist."

"I can see what you mean. I've always thought humans ruin everything."

"I guess so," he answered after mulling over the thought.

"And society?"

"Treated officers like they were some sort of..."

"Super hero?"

"I have not heard the expression, but I think you have the correct meaning. The North won the battle and swooned over the leaders."

"Are you saying they didn't earn it?"

"We gave orders that got men killed."

There, one reason for PTSD. If this actually happened that is. *Oh, come on Dixie, enjoy this for the story that it is, the history that he knows, has read about, and is unveiling.*

"Did you not do the best you could in an impossible situation? That's the kind of steadfast man you are. Now, no swooning here, but didn't you do everything humanly possible to make the right decision? That takes it out of your hands and into God's."

"I do not even know if God was in that hellish place."

"He was. He is everywhere. You should know that better than me."

"Thanks for being practical…and not swooning."

"I can swoon if you want."

"Maybe later." James smiled again, making her more than happy that she made it happen amongst a serious conversation. Whatever their relationship, it helped open up this man.

Again, the woman brought out hidden words within him and without much effort. She made him smile as well. If she ever made it out of here, he would miss the sprite.

"Something just occurred to me," Dixie said.

Her smile made him curious. "Do I dare ask what?"

"How much weight can the Morgan carry?"

"A lot."

"Perhaps as much as my weight and your weight together?"

"Yes, why?"

Dixie laughed from somewhere deep inside and it bubbled up. He would not stop her flow of laughter for anything.

She put her hands on her knees, making the boots seem so out of place on her, adding to his lightheartedness.

"We are not riding together because it would not be proper."

She could make him stupid too, looks like. Now he'd have to work at defending himself. "Do you not remember that you said you wanted to walk for a while?"

"I did say that, yes. But, you walked all that way, when you could have been more comfortable."

"I would not have been comfortable with you so close." There he had said it, and it would have to be all right.

After smiling an ear-to-ear smile, she said. "You're a good man, James."

"Thank you, Dixie, not from the south."

Dixie chuckled as she pushed through brush and flapping limbs. He couldn't help but smile as well.

At length, he looked at his timepiece and said, "After walking awhile in the wilderness the scenery can start looking the same."

"You're not trying to discourage me, are you?"

He wanted to prepare her for disappointment, but could not tell her that at the moment. Soon enough she would see for herself.

"Remember you can come visit me any time. I'd like to get to know you better in Boise."

"Dare I ask what getting to know you better means? I already know you."

"This is it!" Dixie walked through the clearing and stopped, flopped on the ground of the hillside and looked up at the sky. The Morgan pulled away, taking advantage of the lull and munched on grass.

"So you say this is where you woke up?"

"Where I came to. I was unconscious."

"Are you sure this is the place?"

"Yes." She sat up. "Now, if someone carried me here, then I need to look in each direction. Certainly, I wouldn't be carried too far, don't you think?"

"That would be logical, I would presume." Yet, he knew logic and Dixie did not always mix.

Dixie had made it this far and could not lose hope. She stood and then marched up the hill.

"You can see up the hill, Dixie."

"Yes, I know, but maybe I can see something from up there."

From her position, she didn't have a complete view, as trees obstructed parts of the scenery. After some time of moving about, she didn't see a cave, or a car, and her heart beat as if it had suddenly grown in size. She'd left the keys in the car, not remembering her belief that people ruin everything."

Below, James, leaning out from the underside of a large tree, shook his head.

Sitting down, Dixie put her face in her hands and tried to think beyond this site, in which she hadn't let herself do until now.

She'd driven through the small town of Sumpter on her way to the cave. Along the short main street, she passed a gas station, a log motel and small general store. There, she could call for help and stay overnight if she had to wait for her father or mother to arrive.

"I am sorry this did not work," he said. So into her own thoughts, she hadn't heard him approach.

She nodded, thankful he didn't say, "I told you so."

"What would you like to do now?" he asked, in a quiet voice.

Feeling a lump in her throat, Dixie knew she couldn't talk about it without crying. Instead she said, "Let's pull out that jerky stuff and eat. Besides, we need a break from traveling."

Chapter 7

If James did not know it before, he knew now that Dixie believed what she said about where she had been and the car she claimed to have. Her bottom lip trembled between bites and she looked at everything except him. Momentarily, he felt sorry for the sprite until her chin went up in response to the pep talk he figured she gave herself.

"James, can you, or someone you trust, guide me to Sumpter tomorrow? You can leave me in town; I know I can make it home from there."

James studied Dixie's face and considered her words.

She took a deep breath and said, "I have no money to pay you now, but I can promise that the ground below me is where you need to dig for gold."

After a quick glance around the area, with geological clues in mind, he said, "Are you sure?"

"Yes. As I said before, I came to do a newspaper article on the nugget found here. The largest recovered in many, many years."

He did not look for gold here, no one else apparently did either, yet see seemed so earnest. "Huh."

"I'm thinking that the property owner changed his mind about telling me, worrying others would swarm the area. Next, I saw a man murdered, so I kept my mouth shut. I understood the violence was due to others realizing a payday, and certainly a woman was not going to get the best of them. Now, I have nothing to lose by telling you. If a man can keep a secret, you can. Just watch your back and keep safe. Please."

James had to smile at her last words, as he had been watching his back for a long time now.

He wanted to give her the benefit of the doubt, but still needed to clarify her facts. "So, the nugget was simply lying right here?"

"No, silly, it's been a long time since gold was spotted that way. Besides searching the waterbeds, gold is found in the ground, probably the deeper down the better. It would make sense for me to believe the owner found it somewhere in the tunnel he dug out."

"There is a tunnel around here?" He had not seen nor heard of it.

"I thought I told you that," she said, with furrowed brow. "Put on your listening ears."

"My listening ears?" A laugh escaped from his gut before he even realized.

"Shhh! You don't want to bring others here. We should leave."

Yes, they should get back, but not because of the secret gold. "You do not have to bribe me with stories of gold, Dixie. I will take you to Sumpter, anyway."

"You don't believe me, I can tell. But I'm telling you the truth."

***

They didn't quite make it back to the cabin. James stopped at the Blacksmith's shop and took a seat at the table. Dixie watched him take pieces of leather and mend a harness.

"You don't have to babysit me. I can take Morgan and go to the cabin. Perhaps I can straighten it up."

He shook his head. "As I am sure you have noticed, this is a man's town. Too dangerous for a sprite like you."

In response to her pouting lip, he said, "You are not to name my horse."

"So shoot me, I gave him a generic name. He is a Morgan horse after all."

"Shoot you?" He asked with a chuckle.

"You know what I mean. And I'm going to kiss *Morgan* right smack on the forehead when you're not looking."

"Free with your kisses, you are," he said, and winked at her.

Dixie smiled and then looked down shyly. He caught her off guard by flirting. At length, she said, "I'm impressed with your work skills. Where did you learn to work leather like that?"

"My father helped build Oregon and I could not very well do his job, so he introduced me to a leatherman and I became his apprentice."

"You couldn't learn carpentry?"

"What? No, my father did not build cabins. He wore a suit and helped grow the business of Oregon."

"Kind of like a CEO, then?"

He gave her that look and then nodded his head. Like at the moment it was easier to nod than to ask her what CEO stood for.

"So, this is your job in this community?"

"I practiced law, like I said, and saved up some money before I came here. Yet, I need something to do when in short supply of gold. I share this space with the blacksmith, as you know."

No time like the past, she guessed. In the present, his behavior was not unlike dropping out of medical school to become a stand-up comedian.

Speaking candid, because no one else probably would, Dixie said, "This is an awesome skill you have here and admirable that you've started a small business, but you spent a lot of time in college to be an attorney. Don't give up. Living up to your potential is important."

He gave her a half smile, a slightly perturbed one she'd say. "I am an unmarried man without responsibilities and can do as I wish."

He was right, it wasn't her business.

"Speaking of which, why are you not married, caring for children?"

"Haven't found anyone I want to marry. And I'm old fashioned enough to say that I don't want a child without a husband." She had high standards and that was okay.

James put down his work to say, "I should hope you would marry first. Ostracized is the word that comes to mind."

Feeling chastised, and not wanting this feeling from James, she looked down at her hands. It took her a moment to realize she'd not just had a child out of wedlock. She smiled at herself, then watched James's handsome face take on different expressions as he worked. She hoped never to forget his face, ever.

"Have you thought anymore about taking the stage?" he asked.

"Did you change your mind about taking me to Sumpter?" she asked, and held her breath.

"No, I can take you to Sumpter. As I said, I need supplies. I am only checking to see if you have considered all of your options."

The stage could very well circle around and come back to Cracker, never leaving the area like some sort of horror movie. "I have thought about it repeatedly and would prefer you to take me to Sumpter."

***

The moon glowed as they walked back to the cabin with Morgan trailing behind.

"I don't think I've ever seen such big stars," said Dixie.

"They are beautiful, when you get a peek through the smoke that is. Thank you for waiting for me at the shop."

"I didn't mind watching you. I mean watching you work."

"You said that on purpose, did you not?" he asked with a smile.

"I did, yes. And thanks for the food. Where did you find the jerky? It's good."

"I think it is made in Boston. At least it comes from there."

"Good. American made."

He gave her a quizzical look. It gladdened her heart that he'd almost stopped asking about anything that had to do with the modern day. It grew tiresome answering questions for both of them, but probably more so for James as he had to be on his toes twenty-four-seven to stay within the guidelines of this place.

As they traveled up the slope to the cabin she heard a wolf whistle.

"Not everyone has retired for the night, I see."

"I feel like a celebrity with all this attention," she said with a chuckle.

"A celebrity?"

She stopped and thought for a moment. "Like an actor in a Shakespearean play, I guess."

"I think I understand what you mean. I suppose so, but take this as yet another reminder to not go off on your own."

"No, I'll continue to be shackled to you and at your mercy."

"You have a vulgar mouth, woman," he said, but his smile belied the words.

She smiled, too, happy to enjoy his company for tomorrow she'd make it home to Boise. So pleased at the prospect, she turned and kissed Morgan on the forehead. "Good-night, beautiful Morgan."

"Hey," said James.

"You don't have to love him, but I can."

James appeared to ignore her as he knocked some hay off a makeshift bale. Morgan waited for James to fasten him to the cabin before he took his first bite. The homemade chain gave him ample room to lie down when ready. As she walked into the cabin she heard Morgan's puffs of breath as he ate.

In short order they both climbed under the blankets in their respective spots of the night before. Dixie, now exhausted, couldn't hold back what was on her mind, even though contentious. "James?"

"Huh?" He sounded just as drowsy.

"Are you allowed to leave this place, I mean Cracker, when you want to?"

After a moment, he said, "Yes, of course."

"I want you to come see me in Boise."

"You have said that before."

"Meaning, I'm serious." She set up, and turned even though she couldn't read his expression in the dark. "You can think of your time away as a vacation. You don't have to think of us as a couple or with any kind of commitment, if that's what makes you hesitant."

"That is a long way to go for a vacation."

"By horse, you mean?" she asked as more of a statement than a question. Obviously, he didn't want to come. People didn't generally travel that far by horse anymore. After his silence, she said, "I understand. I do. I'll not ask you about Boise again."

"You do not understand. No matter what I feel for you, I will not be traveling to Boise any time soon."

She lay back down. "I see."

"You must promise me that you will never speak to a man this way again, except to a fiance or husband. Certainly, with words such as these, you will be taken advantage of. You need a good man to marry you, place you in his home where you will be safe and within his care. Be not burdened with someone like me who is not ready." He took a breath and continued, "You are older, mid-twenties, but I think a widower would be very interested in you."

"Are you crazy?" she shouted and threw some sort of small tool at him. It sounded like it hit the wall above his head.

In one second he held her arms down above her head. "You do not throw things at people who are trying to help you. Just because you are not getting what you want does not justify your actions."

"It's not because I'm not getting what I want. It's because you are belittling me as a woman, telling me I'm not fit for anything but marriage and life under some man's thumb. Those are harsh words, Mister."

He let go of her hands and leaned back on his haunches. "Who filled your head with this nonsense?"

Two could play this game. "Who filled your head with this nonsense?" Since she caught him off guard, she added, "Would you want your daughter to go through the simple life you just imagined for me?"

"That is not a simple life. Having a family is a fine thing."

"I agree one-hundred percent with that statement. But what if your daughter didn't find the right man and wanted to do something else for a while, like have a job she enjoyed doing?"

"You mean because she looks like me and not her beautiful mother?" he asked.

James tried to break the tension by using humor, she knew, but still she had to get her feelings out. "Her life should be about feeling good about her face and body, no matter if she looks like you, and she should know who she is as a person. If she's not viewing herself that way, then she's not ready to get married."

"Does it not make you feel beautiful when a man kisses you?"

"Not really, because I could have a bag over my head, and a young man could still want to kiss me."

James laughed so hard that he went to all fours.

"A man can't truly save a woman. She has to save herself first," she said, leaning toward him.

"I do not know about that, because something about you makes me want to be a better man. A man like I used to be."

Even though she wanted to believe this to be true, she replied, "Don't just placate me, so I will shut up and go to sleep."

"No. It is true."

"I can't be nothing without a man."

She could almost feel the wheels in his head turning until he said, "Of course I would want my daughter to feel this way about herself. I think we should all feel like this, both man and woman for that matter. As you know, at this time people are not of this notion. That is not how society thinks and those very thoughts will get you scorned."

"But -"

"No more on this. Go to sleep."

"How about a kiss good-night?"

He rose to his feet and moved away. "You are incorrigible," he said, but chuckled.

Dixie settled back down into the blanket, smiling, because she liked having enough power over this man to make him smile and laugh. That was a fine thing for such a taciturn man.

Chapter 8

At sunrise, James gathered a few supplies for the day and unhitched the horse. Morgan shook his head and marched his feet from side to side, ready for exercise.

Others moved about the town, getting an early start on mining before the heat of the day. He took the celebrity, as Dixie called herself, and walked among them.

"Would you like to ride first?" he asked Dixie.

"Since you are freshest in the morning, I'll ride."

He nodded and helped her swing onto the saddle.

"You make riding a horse look so easy," she said, holding onto the saddle horn to steady herself.

"It is so when you have lived on them for as many years as I have."

"You're a good man, James."

"You have said that before and that is enough, Dixie. I am not your dog that you can pat on the head and murmur sweet things over."

"Oh, *come on*. I'm thankful you're taking the time to help me."

He had not felt like a good man since before the war and may never do so again. "A thank you is sufficient."

"I'm going to get some jerky and take it home with me."

"I get tired of it myself. I miss a home cooked meal."

"For something different, we can eat at a restaurant in Sumpter. I know I passed one driving through."

Driving through, he thought, *she does not let up.*

"It will be so nice to have a bath. I just wish I had clean jeans to change into."

"The skirt you packed is sufficient," he said firmly.

He thought she rolled her eyes, but it happened so fast he was not sure.

"When I can, I will repay you for the clothes and extra for the food."

"Not necessary. Think of it as hospitality."

"You're a good- Sorry."

"Humph."

"I'm going to miss sleeping with you," she said in a wistful tone of voice.

James looked around for others in ear shot, but no one was close enough to hear.

"Dixie," he replied, his voice rising on the last syllable of her name. Turning toward her he saw a smile on her face and an erect posture, and he knew she was not done taunting him. "Why do you do that to me?"

"Because it's fun. And true. It's okay to be human, stuffed shirt."

Appalled at her words, he said, "Am I not human?"

She leaned over and touched his arm. When she had his attention, she said in a soft voice, "You're so careful to do the right thing, as if it could make up for whatever happened in the war. Loosen up. There isn't a better man than you, Mister."

James picked up a step and pulled Morgan with him. *How dare she say that?* She knew not one thing about what he went through. What he still went through. He had experienced hell, yet she judged so lightly.

"I'm sorry, James. I meant those words to be a compliment. They just fell out of my mouth. I'm just so tired and weary of not being home. Don't let me get to you. *Please.*"

It was too soon to forgive her. Way too soon, and a quiet trip suited him well.

Dixie knew his anger had to do with the fact that she got close to the truth. He'd served in the Middle East, not as a lieutenant in the Civil War. Pushing real life away wasn't healthy. Not that she knew anything about PTSD, but a monkey knew he couldn't pretend the present didn't exist except for edges of it melded together with a fantasy.

Over and over, she shook her head at her ignorance. He made it more than clear that he didn't want to involve himself in her life. So, then why did she try to get involved in his?

After about a half hour of silence, she said, "I bet you will be glad to get rid of me, and I don't blame you."

"Don't worry, I'll get over it."

Of course he would. Yet, she'd over stepped her boundaries and he, a good man, didn't deserve it.

Dixie felt like a child, impatient to reach their destination. Finally the path widened considerably, but not into a paved road. Wagons made marks on this dirt road, which made sense because behind her set Cracker, 1870.

Chapter 9

"Oh, *no*," Dixie said as they entered Sumpter. Not long ago she'd driven through here, but now the town had turned into the 1800s as well. The buildings, the wooden walkways, people riding on horseback and wagons moving about, all old-fashioned. Fear gripped her chest as she studied women dressed in long dresses and hats, their little girls in bonnets. A city this size could not be kept secret. Why hadn't she heard of this place?

What had happened to her? Did she really hit her head and have amnesia? No, her memories were clear; she lived and worked in Boise and her family did too. The clothes she arrived in helped prove her past if nothing else.

A glance at James confirmed her worries as he'd been watching her, waiting for her to say something.

What could she say? What could she *do*?

They moved forward and stopped near a bath house. Across the street she spotted a post office. Certainly a government agency couldn't be anything but accurate, following strict guidelines.

"James, can you wait for me here? I'd like to go into the post office."

He nodded, still observing her closely. Actually, many eyes followed her, studying her pants, shoes, and James's shirt that covered more than half her body. Her heart beat hard and a headache had made its way to the back of her head.

After pushing through the large doors of the entrance, she moved to the back of the building to observe. She spotted a calendar near a narrow table where two men stood writing. She moved between the men and noted large print dating the calendar 1870.

Turning away, she saw costumers receiving change, bills not familiar to her.

"Is this a federal post office," she asked a man behind the counter.

"Why yes, of course," he answered, perusing her attire.

"Thank you."

Something was horribly wrong. Nothing made sense. Sure, she'd read of scientific work toward time travel to the future, but nothing in regards to the past. Not possible to go back in time, they'd said. If she'd entered into the cave and literally fell into the past, then she had no parents, no friends, and no job. She could have counted on James as a friend, but her candid mouth ruined it with him. What kind of friend was she anyway?

Her possessions added to a broken watch, diamond earrings, clasp for her hair, boots, a blouse and a skirt. Despite her pitiful circumstances, she had to pull herself together and make this work.

Outside, James watched her approach. She put her shoulders back and chin up, more for her benefit than his.

When Dixie came out of the post office, James saw fear etched in her pale face. Something serious had happened to her in a public place, while otherwise calm people came in and out. Still, he braced himself for battle as he had done numerous times in the past.

Dixie had ample time to prove to him she was not the type to be overly fearful, or embarrassed. Something had scared the wits out of her.

"How did it go?" he asked, then took in a breath, waiting for her answer.

Of course, James referred to what she did inside the post office, but she'd keep this bit of knowledge to herself or expect to be put in some kind of a horrible house for the mentally insane.

"I won't be going to Fort Boise after all," she tried very hard to say nonchalantly. "My job is no longer available, so I need to find a job here."

His eyebrows nearly touched his nose, and she had to look away to keep a lump from forming in her throat. She focused on the bathhouse. Yes, she'd take a nice serene bath while thinking this out.

"I'd like to take a bath now, if I may."

"Of course." He gave her a few coins and searched through his pack for her new clothes. Dixie detested that she couldn't pay her way and felt like a child taking money from a parent.

"When you are done, wait on the front bench. I have some business to attend to."

"Sure."

Inside, she noticed two women working in the front, one passing out soap and towels. She'd die doing something like this and hoped she could get a job at the newspaper office in town.

The other women said something about sharing the bath water after someone else. "What?" she asked, unable to believe what she heard.

"You can choose fresh hot water, or the cheaper way is to share bath water with someone finished before you."

The good old days were not so good, she decided. "Fresh water, please."

While sitting and appreciating her fresh bath water, she thought about what a newspaper job in 1870 could entail. James said he'd never seen a woman working at a newspaper office. Well, there had to be a first. As she leaned back the best she could in a metal tub, she considered her new life's limitations. Still, the earrings could get her a room to rent until she could find work.

In the past, she'd thought of her parents in times of trouble. Now, she realized, they hadn't even been born. Tears ran down her cheeks over the possibility of never seeing them again.

***

When James found Dixie, he said, "The clothes fit you well."

Suddenly her relationship with him had changed, making her feel like a stranger again. She mustered a smile and said, "Good, because this will have to do. At least I was able to put my hair back in a French braid."

"You look very nice." After an awkward moment, he said, "My turn to scrub off the dirt. The horse will be fine tethered there. Please wait here."

She nodded and sat down on the bench, while thinking this could give her at least ten minutes to look around town. Although not much time, it was a task she'd like to do alone.

"Excuse me," she asked a man walking by. "Can you tell me the way to the newspaper office?"

He touched his hat in greeting. "You are in luck, it is only around the corner on Mill Street."

Dixie grabbed her rolled up clothes and whipped around the corner, her feet pounding the wooden boards of the walkway. When she found the building, she walked across the street and looked in the window. James was right, only men working here. Still, she studied the machines as best she could through the window.

Mentally, she searched her mind for a makeshift verbal resume, so she'd appear professional and worth hiring. What work could she do? For that matter, what could she do without a computer?

She set her roll of clothes on the ground in front of the office. On second thought, she picked them up and pushed them as far as she could back along her side. She didn't want to lose the diamonds in her pockets or the change of clothes. Although not in style, perhaps she could wear her jeans inside her rented room.

At the door, she heard the clicking of typewriters and the harsh movement of a revolving printing machine. It sounded like two men were discussing an article that needed editing.

Finally, her heart rose. She could edit, that she was sure of.

"Good day, sir," Dixie said and stuck out her hand to the man sitting at the largest desk.

He stood and shook her outstretched hand. "Good day, ma'am. What can I do for you?"

"I'm looking for employment, and would love to work at your newspaper."

After a moment, he said, "I am sorry but we sweep our own floors, and attend to all the cleaning right now."

Her heart took a dive. "No, I am an excellent editor; I can look over your articles. I can type and am willing to learn to manage any type of machinery you have."

The men in the office turned toward her as one.

"That is remarkable since the typewriter was only just invented, but we have enough employees at this time.

Still, ma'am, you should know that our editing jobs go to men who need to provide for their families."

With an enormous effort she held her tongue, knowing that someday she may need one of these men for a job down the line.

"Thank you for your time." She smiled her best smile and turned to leave. Out of sight, she ran down the wooden walk, the exercise and the noise helping to calm her.

"Is someone chasing you?" James asked, glaring behind her.

"No, no, nothing like that. I'm okay."

He looked doubtful, so she said, "You clean up real nice."

He smiled, then turned serious as he said, "When you were in the bath house, I did some checking around, and it looks to me like you have only two living options."

After moving her out of earshot of anyone walking by, he continued, "There is a woman named Marie Chastain who can take you in as a boarder."

"Oh?" she asked, filling with much needed hope.

"It is not all good, Dixie. Her boarding house is near a brothel in a questionable section of town."

"Well then, I can find another boarding house."

"No, it is not that easy. She is the only one who will take on a single woman at this time."

"Oh," she replied in a small voice.

"That is because of the men, the miners, returning to town looking for a woman. Not all wish to use a brothel. Men coming and going interferes with the other boarder's peaceful lifestyle and could lead to questionable clientele."

Refusing housing due to the sex of the person, she thought. This would never happen in the future without a lawsuit, which didn't help her to think about today.

"There is a job," he added quickly.

"A job?" she asked, her voice returning to its normal pitch.

"A laundry here in Sumpter needs a woman, which is work, but hard on the hands and back."

Another tough reminder that she now lived in 1870 without appliances that made labor much easier. "So if living here and working at a laundry is one choice, what is the other?"

"Before I talk about the other option, I want you to tell me precisely what happened to you in the post office."

The moment of truth. Dixie sighed, then partially unrolled her clothes. "I need to get something out of my pocket." After finding what she needed she said, "Just before you originally found me, I was wearing this watch. I want you to look at it."

"This is a watch? It is cracked," he said, matter-of-factly.

"Look closer, at the numbers."

He frowned as he concentrated. "I see 2017-06-30. I do not understand what that means."

"The six stands for the month of June. The thirty is the thirtieth day of June."

When she hesitated, he asked, "And what is two-thousand-seventeen?"

"When I awakened, after being in a tunnel, I saw that my watch had stopped precisely at the time of my transport, at ten-fifteen in the morning, in the year twenty-seventeen."

"I have not seen a timepiece such as this before."

Was he not hearing her? "That's because they haven't been invented yet."

Finally his eyes met hers, certainly looking for any sign of humor communicated in body language.

"You know, I wouldn't believe it either. But you know how we have a hard time communicating? You don't always know what I'm talking about. My pants, for example, I called them jeans. A…my car, you don't know what that is. Anyway, it appears to be modern anachronisms I'm using, you know, associated with a particular period in time."

James crossed his arms and continued to stare at her, like an unidentified bug under a microscope. So, she continued to talk. "Until I entered the post office, I thought that Cracker was some sort of a group of people wanting to live in a certain time period, the 1800s to be specific."

"Why would anyone choose to do that?"

"That was exactly the way I felt at the time, and why I wasn't sympathetic to your service in the Civil War. I thought you made everything up and had some sort of unwritten code to stay within the boundary of the time period."

His eyes narrowed. "If I was going to make something up, which I would not do, I certainly would not pick a wartime conversation. I am appalled that you think I would."

"I know that now. I'm sorry." Like a huge giant hand, fear gripped her chest. She felt adrenaline charge every cell in her body when she realized she hadn't done anything to make James want to help her now.

He was wrong, she did trust him. She reached back into her pocket. "I have something else to show you. I have some earrings. See?"

James studied the earrings with wide eyes. "Are these diamonds?"

She watched him roll them around in his palm. "Yes. Together they make two carats. My parents gave these to me when I graduated from college."

"How do they fit on your ears? There must be a piece missing."

Dixie put a loose stand of hair behind an ear. "See the tiny hole in the bottom of my earlobe?"

"A...yes. It is small, but I see it."

Despite being upset, she liked the feel of his warm fingers on her ear. A pang in the bottom of her gut told her she didn't want to leave him, but had no choice. "Most women of my time wear pierced earrings. They stay on the ear better."

"Understood, but you should not be showing these to anyone. They have great value."

She nodded and a tear threatened to spill.

"What do these things have to do with me?" he asked, softly.

"When you took a bath, I went to the newspaper office. Seems they don't hire women at this time. So, perhaps you can help me trade these in for money. I need something to live on. I don't know what they are worth in 1870 and don't want to be taken advantage of in any way."

Dixie started to cry and it disturbed him deeply. Surprisingly so. He had seen mentally ill people before and it was not a stretch of the imagination to deem them so. The only thing delusional about Dixie was her words, which she apparently believed on account of the tears and anxiousness.

A different kind of woman, she shied of no one, spoke her mind when a lady should not and added overbold reddish stripes to her hair. However, her brains, logic and good health belied a wanton woman.

Something had happened to her in that cave, he would give her that. The watch and her earrings were clearly nothing he had ever seen in any social circle.

"Certainly, you do not want to lose this gift from your parents."

She took a deep breath. "I am thankful I have something for an emergency."

He understood what she meant. Still, he had one more plan to present to Dixie. "I cannot leave you alone in Cracker or Sumpter, Dixie."

She slanted her head and gave him a wistful smile. "You're a good man, James, but you owe me nothing."

Again, she said he was a good man. He wanted to be a man of integrity more than anything, and especially wanted to live up to what she thought of him. In his mind, there was only one way to do that. "Come around the corner of the building, Dixie."

Dixie looked up at him like she feared he would take the earrings and run. For good measure he placed them in her hand. Just around the corner, he got down on one knee and took her hand.

"Will you marry me, Dixie Lea?"

She pulled up on his hand to no avail. "Don't be funny, James."

"I am not being funny. You are the first woman since the war that has made me even think of marriage."

"Don't be thinking I'm some needy woman that can't stand on her own, because I'm not."

"Your independence is something I like about you. As a matter-of-fact, I think I may need you."

Out of the corner of Dixie's eye, a woman walked by with children trailing behind her. The woman had a basketball-shaped belly and eight children. This was a warning if she'd ever seen one.

"Do you want children, James?"

"Yes."

She put a hand on her cheek, after realizing any type of effective contraceptive was probably not invented yet.

He stood. "You do not want children, Dixie?"

"Yes, but I'd only thought about having two children."

James still had a hold of her hand and looked sincere, which added to her confusion. She took a deep breath, and considered how surreal this all seemed. In the last hour or so, she found out she lived in another century, overwhelming by itself, and now she had to make major decisions in a small amount of time.

The only one Dixie could count on was James, but even though attracted to him, she couldn't marry someone out of need.

He cleared his throat, obviously uncomfortable when he said, "How many children we have, or do not have, is a discussion that needs to be made of course."

"Yes, but I don't even know if we have a choice in how many children we have. A…it happens automatically when a couple is close."

He nodded.

Dixie's hands shook like leaves in a breeze as she slipped in and out of anxiousness. Still, she had to speak up for her herself, her welfare. "I hope you will understand that I can't make a decision right this moment. I'm overwhelmed with where I am right now, never returning to my home, not sure what to do. I need a few days to process all this. I'm not saying I won't marry you, but we *both* need to take a little time before we commit to this. Surely you see that, don't you?"

"I see you need time. Are you willing to return with me to Cracker, then?"

"That I know I can do. Perhaps I can help you with something to earn my keep."

He nodded, then guided her to the horse. Her shaking hands prevented her from grabbing the saddle firmly, so James hiked her up and then sat behind her.

Thankful that someone had a hold of her, she leaned back into him and he steadied her as if he knew she needed the contact.

Chapter 10

As Morgan moved along toward Cracker, James took an inconspicuous sniff of Dixie's clean hair for the hundredth time and thought about what he had asked of her.

She was right not to jump into marriage. For one, he needed to think about what he wanted to do for a permanent job and then settle down and do it. Only then would he be good husband material.

Not that he blamed himself; he had not met anyone he wanted to marry until Dixie. This was a worry in itself as the woman had shown signs of confusion, to say the least.

"Tell me something of your time, Dixie," he said into her ear.

"Water costs two dollars a bottle at the airport."

He chuckled. "You pay for water? That is hardly progress."

She couldn't agree more, and laughed at the irony.

"And what is an air port?"

"Well let's see. Two men, the Wright brothers, studied the flight of birds and tried to make some type of object that could simulate the movement of birds in flight." She flapped her arms.

"Too heavy to work."

She nodded. "Still, they kept drawing plans and after several attempts they were able to produce the first plane that could be controlled with an engine."

"Oh? When did that happen?"

I think at the last part of the eighteenth century or early 1900s. So, I expect the brothers were born some time this decade then."

"What would be the use of such an instrument?"

She tried to turn back toward him, to look in his face. He struggled with whether to kiss her cheek or search for lunacy in her features.

"To carry people from one place to another in a timely manner, is the value. I know this sounds far-fetched, but so much has changed, especially from the early nineteen-hundreds. And better modes of travel are one of the first great inventions."

After a moment of silence, she said, "Now don't be thinking I'm an alien from outer space."

"No, it did not cross my mind." In a moment, he said, "Should I?"

"No," she said, irritated.

Time travel and a sizable object that could take people safely into the air did not seem feasible. James considered what he knew about Dixie.

When they met, she told him she arrived that morning from Fort Boise. As if dropped down into a strange place, she knew nothing about the area. Even though miles from home, she had not traveled long because she smelled of flowers, freshly clean and clothed, and not within walking distance from a bath house. That alone was a mystery.

James had never met a woman quite like her whether rich or poor in regards to beliefs about life. She appeared to be of wealth, free of knowing anything about how to provide her daily sustenance. But, even well-heeled, she would have some idea.

The forwardness she demonstrated around him was questionable. She clearly did not act like a spinster, but one eager to latch onto a man. Yet, she clearly liked her independence, confident and proud to be so.

Her confidence, her sense of self-esteem did not fit with someone roaming the forest for survival. All she wanted from the beginning was to get back home to her family and job. Whether she ever saw him again was not her goal, however, he wished it to be so.

Dixie cleared her throat. "Tell me what *you* think will happen in the future?"

"That is a good question. The Bible says that there will always be war or rumors of war."

"That proves to be true."

He could have gone forever without knowing that, he realized. "I think I have more wishes than anything else."

"That's just it. Unless you are a hopeful dedicated scientist, or an innovator, you can't know what the future will bring. Most can't just pull an idea out of the air."

"What do you mean by innovator?"

"A…someone who introduces some sort of helpful device or a new way of doing something, I suppose."

"And there are many innovators in the future?"

"Yes, but there are a lot more people as well. If people have a dozen kids each generation, that's what happens," she said simply, not in judgment.

"I imagine that will continue to happen," he returned.

"No, at least not in most countries. If possible, women can choose whether to have a job or stay home with their family. They have a choice whether to have children or not."

"How can most women *not* have children?"

"A scientist, probably scientists, came up with a way, ways, to keep a woman from getting pregnant."

"Huh. That helps me understand you and your choices a bit better."

She leaned forward, straightened her back. "You sound like you're starting to believe me," she said with a rising voice of hope.

"There is a lot I do not understand at this point."

She leaned back. "In the future attorneys are not always presented in a favorable light."

He knew Dixie tried to lash back after his last comment and while wanting to express amusement, thought better of it. Instead he said, "How can it be otherwise? *That* is imaginable."

Although exhausted, Dixie didn't think she'd sleep tonight. Propping herself against the outside of the cabin, she watched James take the saddle and bag off Morgan. She felt sorry for the horse and fetched the amount of oats that James usually gave him.

"There you go Morgan. Thanks for the ride, sweetheart."

"You are welcome," said James.

"I was talking to Morgan."

He turned toward her. "You should not name the horse."

"I already did. He deserves some TLC."

"What is TLC?"

"Tender loving care."

"Is that what people in your time give to horses?"

She crossed her arms, feeling the cold as the sun moved west. "Well, if a horse is not properly cared for then they are considered abused and the owner will lose the animal. That applies to dogs and cats as well."

"These days a horse is needed for travel, so abuse is not usually a concern. Until we fly in the air, that is."

"I hope you're not making fun of me."

"No, I am not."

To spite him, Dixie leaned forward and kissed Morgan on the nose. She turned to look back at James on her way in the door and caught him smiling to himself.

Inside she looked around wondering how she could help prepare food for the two of them, especially since James had a job and she didn't. She hadn't a clue.

"When will your stove arrive?" she asked him when he came through the door.

"I am told this week."

"I'm just thinking about how and what I can cook. I don't know how to operate a wood burning stove, but I've seen them in antique stores. I can learn."

He nodded.

"I used to eat a lot of salads."

"Oh? What do you mean by salads?" he asked.

"A bowl of mixed vegetables. Sometimes I add pasta and other times I add chopped poultry or meats."

"Pasta?"

"Oh. It's a...flour, water and egg mixture that is stretched, cut and boiled."

"When you say vegetables, it sounds like you eat summer foods to me."

"In my century, a person is able to get just about any food, fruit or vegetable, at any time and any place in America."

"How can that be?" he asked without malice in his tone, only curiosity and maybe a touch of hope.

"Well, with improved modes of travel, food preservation and availability have improved greatly. I wish now I would've been more thankful for each bite."

She appreciated his listening to her like a friend, without judgment, and her emotions welled up. After a moment of silence to collect herself, she said, "Has aluminum foil been invented for cooking yet?"

"I do not know what that is, so I think not."

She snapped her fingers. "Darn."

"You want to darn something?"

"A…no, that is a saying, an expression of dismay."

"Oh. Do not worry; I have lived some years without anyone cooking for me."

She nodded.

"Hungry?"

"Yes."

"How about some bread, canned salt pork and beans?" he asked.

She smiled. "That seems like a feast right now."

James made her feel like everything would be all right. Even more tempting than food was the desire to marry such a man. Still she couldn't succumb to emotion or need, but had to fully think things out.

As they lay down for the night in their respective places, Dixie felt like she might be able to sleep after all, her bones weary enough after stressing and jumbling around on a horse for hours.

"Good-night," she said.

"Sleep. Do not worry about a thing this night."

Chapter 11

James woke up before first light, and moved quietly to keep from waking Dixie. Perhaps peace and rest could help her come to grips with reality as she now knew it.

Time travel did not make sense to him, but after each minute that passed her lack of knowledge of how to live spoke volumes of truth. Her whole existence indicated a member of royalty locked away in a tower, equally unlikely.

Along those lines, he set out food to feed her until he returned from a day of work at the leather shop. He would take her to the store in late afternoon.

Dixie woke with a start and dismay flooded her senses when she took in her surroundings. Sitting up, she looked across the room and panicked until she realized James wouldn't leave without his bedroll and belongings. He had a job and a cabin to finish building.

She lay in bed for some time trying to figure out the next steps in her life and came up with nothing concrete. Thankfully, she knew James would not cast her out of his home, yet it concerned her that he would take on a crazy woman with nothing to offer. James could be the crazy one, she knew, as he wanted to marry a woman just because of need. Certainly he had his own problems to sort through himself.

One thing she had to do was find a way to make money or at least to contribute to her room and board.

For the first time in her adult life she realized she couldn't fix her circumstances, so she bent her head in prayer. Only God knew why she was here. Now it was up to Him to get her through this and help her understand why she lingered in 1870.

She dressed, folded her bedding and then reached for the other bedroll when she heard a knock at the door. With a hand on her chest, she wondered if she should open the door. James didn't tell her what to do. After reminding herself she could make choices on her own, she stepped to the edge of the boarded window and saw a man with some metal and aluminum items. It looked pretty harmless to her.

"Hello ma'am. A good morning to you."

"Hello."

"I understand that you do not have many items of your own and thought you could use these. I know you will feel more comfortable with the things you need to run your household."

To her it looked like he brought a load of garbage instead of needed items. When she hesitated he said, "I can see that you are confused. Do not be alarmed, I will explain."

She nodded.

"The whiskey barrel here is good for catchin' the rain water, which is good for washin' the clothes and your hair. Soft water, you know. You can put 'em at the edge of your cabin. Another use is to store food in 'em. Mice cannot get in vera well, you see. Also you can make furniture out of 'em."

Made sense, she supposed. Dixie doubted the old kerosene cans were much good, still she asked, "What are the cans for?"

His eyebrows came together, probably in concern, "Feed chickens out of 'em is one thing. They can be used for many things, ma'am. Your man can prob'ly tell you more."

She hesitated, then nodded.

"Here is an old almanac for the recipes. My wife thought I needed this, but I cannot cook vera well. The newspaper can paper your house. Thought you might make curtains out of the flour sack. You need to gather more of 'em course."

What could she say, without seeming rude? "Well...a...thank you, Mr - "

"Cranston," he finished. He looked familiar but she couldn't place the name. In a second, she remembered she didn't know anyone in this century besides Stephen and James. He just had a common face.

"I will be a goin' now." He bowed and stepped backwards, before turning to leave.

She looked at the pile of things at the door. Was he for real? Was this how people lived these days? However dumbfounded, she admired his versatility, but certainly they weren't so poor that they would need these things. Dixie also realized she thought of herself and James in plural terms which threw her off balance, too.

***

Cranston stood on Main Street, looked back at the Brogan cabin and considered the woman within. Mrs. Brogan had a natural beauty to her that didn't need cosmetics to emphasize her best features. It was not a stretch of the imagination to realize what Brogan saw in her. As a matter-of-fact she had to be used to getting what she wanted in life from the men around her.

A good woman, he doubted. She looked down her nose at the items he brought her in a neighborly fashion. He expected they would stay where they landed until Brogan moved them to a garbage heap somewhere.

He simply wanted to be a friend of the people he deemed important. Yet, when he considered all he'd gone through to get these items and then give them away, his frustration changed to livid anger and he wanted to go back and strangle her, this person who didn't deserve his friendship.

If he decided to take her, end her life, it would be hard to pin him for it with so many men in this town wanting a woman.

Brogan went to work, or mining, most days and wouldn't be around to watch over her. Perhaps she would figure out the value of the items and open the door to him again.

"I am better than her," he said to encourage himself, and moved on down the street.

***

Dixie flipped through the newspapers to find want ads for a suitable job. By the fourth newspaper she lost hope and cried.

At least she could look at the recipes in the almanac, she decided at length. Because of limited ways of keeping food, canned items were her best bet. Perhaps she could find tins of peaches, blueberries and cherries and make pies in James's new stove. Sure, it would take practice to learn how to use the oven, but what else did she have to do?

***

When James returned to the cabin, he immediately sought Dixie's face. He wanted to know her state of mind and hoped she had not decided to walk off after quiet thought.

He nearly fell over an empty kerosene can on his way in and bent to set it aside.

"What is this?"

Dixie stood and gave him a welcoming smile. A good sign.

"A man named Cranston stopped by to give us a few items we might need."

"Oh." He studied her for a moment, before smiling once more. "Even though I do not like the idea of you opening the door to anyone, I see what he thought and it was a kind thing to do."

"Yes, the things have helped me, after Cranston explained some of the uses, that is."

"What? Oh yes, you would not know what these are for." After noting his fidgeting, nervous hands, he asked, "How are you doing? I said prayers for you today."

"Oh? What did you pray for?"

He believed she wanted to know what it is he wanted of her, but it did not matter in the scheme of things.

"I asked that God's will be done."

"What about your will?" she returned, simply.

"It does not matter. If God can keep me alive through the war, then he can tend to your needs."

She took in an extra breath of air with a smile and nodded. He could not ask for more than that, he believed.

Further, she told him of her pie baking plans and if he had not already fallen for her, he did now. Another touch of hope radiated from her being and into her smile.

He had not the heart to tell her she could not make a very good living this way. Certainly, she would sell what she made, but one woman and daylight could only produce so much.

"You have a good work ethic."

"Maybe more of a necessity, I think."

Still, he knew she had one, as it was against everything she believed to make herself comfortable and depend on him for everything. He himself worked hard and fast today to make sure he had more time with her, especially early on with her decision making.

***

At the general store, Dixie studied the hanging bolts of material and the matching notions to go with them. She'd learned about textiles, how to operate a sewing machine, made a bag and a throw pillow in her high school home economics class. At least she'd had an introduction to what may be more than a hobby in this era. Until then, she picked out another skirt and blouse. At least she could interchange them for variety. After picking up some more under things, she moved to where James had stacked food items.

He asked for dark soft soap that was cut from a block and also a bar soap called Ivorine. On the counter James had set rice, beans, cornmeal, lard, saleratus (soda, she believed), cream of tartar, and a darker flour than she was used to seeing. Salted, or dried meats and brine vegetables were aplenty, but when the storekeeper said they didn't have any fruit, she sighed loudly. James, apparently catching her disappointment, said, "We can pick berries in the woods very soon now."

What appeared to be a loaf of sugar, white and brown in layers, was set on the counter next to the long lasting hardtack, or hard bread, made from flour and water of which she'd tasted. She'd had plenty of the cracker-like food already. Last, she grabbed a can of cinnamon thinking she could occasionally sprinkle it and sugar on the hardtack to help get it down and serve as a sort of dessert.

Everything got packed into a galvanized tub, big enough for her to sit in. James, refusing any help from her, lugged it back to the cabin.

He shoved the tub into the side of the cabin and took out the dark soft soap. Next, he stepped outside while she picked up her new clothing and examined it once more.

James stood at the doorway with two large buckets. "Take hold of our dirty clothes and place them in this bucket."

"Sure."

"Come down to the creek with me so I can show you how to wash clothes."

Definitely weird to hear such a statement as she'd washed lots of clothes, but never like this. Standing in front of the tub of supplies, she grabbed the bar of Ivorine and followed behind James.

He'd picked a precise time of day, shortly before dusk, with many exhausted miners returning to their living quarters for the night. She figured with the small amount of clothes they owned, it wouldn't take long.

James found a place down the creek and put the two buckets next to a large rock. He took the dirty clothes out of the bucket, pared off a portion of the dark soap with a knife, took water from the creek, and added the dirty clothes.

He swirled the clothes around with his hands for awhile. "I will start with the shirt on top. He flopped it on the rock, massaged it, and dipped it in the water. "This is to get the dirt out."

"I figured that, Lieutenant," she said, chuckling. "Your turn."

They ended up doing about half and half even though her underwear embarrassed him and he passed it to her to finish. "You're too cute," she said and his eyebrows dipped down in question.

"I like your fairness, is all," she said, only revealing half. "Being fair even after a long day of work."

"I wanted to make sure the laundry was clean," he said and smiled, showing her a touch of humor.

James stood to leave when Dixie took off her shoes, grabbed the Ivorine and jumped into the water, clothes and all."

"What are you doing?"

"Cleaning up." She moved to the other side of another large rock where the water had pooled and completely went under. With the bar, she washed her body as best she could with a skirt and blouse on and then washed her hair.

Even though she didn't really care what James thought, she glanced over to see him sheepishly looking around himself for others, then watched her with intense interest as she moved around in the water.

To think he could be hers forever, she thought and slapped at the water. "Come on in, I'll share the soap."

Dixie, a beautiful, spirited, daring woman and not like any other, James surmised. Further, he moved when she beckoned him. Slowly, he bent to pull off his boots, and she started clapping. "Shirt! Shirt! Shirt!"

He could not help but smile at her antics. "Dixie, stop. You are going to bring the fellows out to watch." Still, he pulled off his shirt and waded in.

"I don't think Ivory soap floats yet, so be careful with it," she said.

"I have used it before."

She made a face and handed him the soap and he washed his hair, everything above his waist, and finally his feet.

A quick kiss to his cheek caught him off guard and he slipped to his bottom.

"That had to hurt," she said and put a hand over her mouth.

"Yes, it did."

"I hope we do this every time we wash clothes."

He shook his head as he moved out of the water, but added a grin. "Do not count on it."

***

At bedtime, Dixie asked James questions about the leather business until his eyelids closed.

"Don't fight it; go to sleep," Dixie said, and smiled at his struggles to be polite and listen. She could have picked a subject more stimulating, but wanted to hear about his work.

James lay on his blanket with hands folded at his chest, and she wondered if she should coax him to get under it, yet didn't want to disturb him. He was a big boy and could fend for himself. She looked closely at the lighted lamp, trying to get used to the workings, before blowing it out.

Dixie listened to James's even breathing until she dozed off. A change in the pattern woke her up. She tensed and pulled her blanket under her chin as she waited for James to say something. No words came, only grunts and harrowing moans that she believed had to do with the war.

She had no idea what a man in the service went through, but was about to see a little slice of it. Dixie got up and moved to his side, careful not to disturb his dreams further. In his ear she said, "It's okay. It's okay. You're here with me. Everything is fine."

He didn't lash out, as she'd expected, but turned his whole body in her direction. Her head dipped until they were nearly face to face. Her hand went to the side of his face and gently caressed him.

"Were you dreaming about the war?" she asked quietly and moved her hand to her side. It was a wonder he hadn't taken to drink and she said so.

He rubbed his face as if to clear his thoughts. "Drinking and the war do not mix well. That is when I learned if you want to stay alive you need to stay alert. Some did otherwise, sad to say."

He took in a breath and moved to his back. "I dreamed you disappeared. That you left me, and went back to your time."

"Really? You know it wasn't all that scary. I entered the tunnel and then found myself on the side of a hill. Not like being attacked by zombies."

"What is a zombie?"

She chuckled. "Never mind. Just a twenty-first century joke."

"Humph."

"I really thought you were dreaming of the war."

"Not this time."

"I don't think of you as being afraid of much." After a quiet moment, she added in a happier tone of voice, "Were you afraid I was going to leave you, big guy?"

Again, quiet.

"Huh, you were. That is so sweet that you worried about me."

James moved to face her again. "It is not that I am afraid, it is that I am starting to get used to having you around."

He tried to say it with humor, but it didn't quite come out that way. When he put his hand on the side of her face, she realized that he truly did care for her. Funny, she thought he only wanted to save her and now she wasn't so sure.

He moved a strand of hair behind her ear. "I am concerned that you let someone in while I was gone."

"I thought it all looked safe enough."

"A...Cranston, did you say?"

"Yes."

"I do not know the man."

"He seemed to know you. At least he mentioned you by name."

"Do not know anyone named Cranston."

"Well, think about it. You have a woman tagging along with you and it's noticed, talked about."

James turned on his back again. "However thoughtful, a decent man, especially here, would wait until the man of the house was home."

"Huh," she said on an outtake of air. "I won't answer the door. Especially if it matters to you that much."

"Thank you."

All that she'd called friend and family were gone, but someone still cared for her. She touched his shoulder in gratitude and realized he'd taken his shirt off sometime during the night. Made sense, it was summer.

His skin was a little moist and heated from the disturbing dream he'd experienced. She started to pull her hand back, but he put his hand on top of hers.

"Thanks for being such a good friend to me. I must seem so pitiful," she said with an awkward chortle.

"I want to be more than a friend. You need to know that every waking moment. Until you make a decision, you best not touch me so."

It took only touching his shoulder to get a reaction such as this and she smiled in the darkness. Also refreshing, since her century would laugh at his principles. She chuckled, thinking of the comparison.

"I do not see the humor, Dixie."

His words shocked her into seriousness, as she didn't want to hurt his feelings in any way. "No, of course you wouldn't. In my mind I compared you to the males in the twenty-first century. I find them lacking in chivalry."

"Then I hope you are glad to be here, in my time."

"*You* are the best thing about my being in this era."

James grabbed the index finger touching his chin and took it to his shoulder while he moved his upper body across her. He gave what started as a sweet kiss, but turned into much more when she took his bottom lip between hers. His firm lips changed to soft as needed, and back again in a knowledgeable way. And back and forth they played this game until James, as if drowning came up for air.

He pulled back further and attempted to steady his breathing. "Certainly you have to see that a decision must be made soon. I am taking a walk."

He was right, she knew, but if only she could make the decision when her life was normal. Then, they would both know that the decision was made correctly. She needed him to understand, but heaven knew that process could take years.

Even so, would he even want her as a whole person? If she wasn't mistaken, James wanted to be a good man, yet it irritated him when she said he was. As if he wanted to make up for something he did in the past, like he could, like duping himself or God into thinking he was a good man by his current actions. It didn't take a rocket scientist to predict that James believed he could right some of the wrongs he'd done in the war by taking her on. At this moment, he was hard pressed to find someone else so in need of everything to survive. She feared marriage would be treated like a business deal for James. Trouble was she really wanted him to love her for who she was not in retribution for his sins.

Stalemate.

Chapter 12

Standing at the door, James spotted a man in the distance, or rather he noticed the glow of the lighted end of a cigarette in the darkness. The hair on the back of his neck seemed to rise as he remembered the dream he woke from.

Something about Cranston bothered him. Perhaps he wanted to get next to one of the few women in town, the only respectable one.

Frankly, it surprised him that no one had tried to get close to her before. Still, he could not take her everywhere he went, especially now that she wanted to bake pies for a living.

He had asked Dixie to make a decision about their relationship, yet his mind constantly went back and forth on whether to be a lawyer, farmer, miner, carpenter, or leather man. He had a hard time making a decision, let alone ask one of her.

At the beginning he proposed to Dixie because he wanted to do something right and good for a change, to make amends for participating in a wretched war. Somehow, she figured this out. However, each moment spent with Dixie made him want her more and more. Now, when he desired to marry her because of love, it made him ashamed that she had to feel this way at all. Just as he had no clue what job to take, he did not know how to make her understand that he truly did love her.

The cigarette no longer glowed in the distance and James turned to go back inside. He needed to have a heart-to-heart talk with Dixie about what they needed to do, because she quite simply risked her life living around some of the West's roughest men.

Inside, he moved as quietly as he could to his bed. He could hear her breath moving in and out in the rhythm of sleep. Their discussion would have to wait until tomorrow after work.

***

Just as James instructed, Dixie stayed away from the door, but wondered how long she could do that before getting cabin fever.

In no time she cleaned and straightened the cabin, finished reading through the almanac and newspapers, and started compiling a grocery list.

In the twenty-first century, Dixie learned that just about any type of home decoration was in fashion. So, she tried to figure out what parts of the newspaper could work for wallpaper, then shook her head and let out a sigh of frustration. She'd love to have some plain old white paint and added it to a list. Certainly some sort of wall covering should be created by now.

For curtains, she didn't want to use flour sacks but hoped to get some basic red-checked gingham material. She'd make some as soon as she purchased a sewing machine. She needed dresses as well, and until she could figure out how to make a dress, she'd buy one with her first business earnings.

She also decided to bake and sell cookies instead of pies as a quicker and more profitable business enterprise. To that extent, she thought long and hard about a chocolate chip cookie recipe, and then listed the ingredients on the list.

Like a silly young bride, James took the foremost part of her mind, and she couldn't wait for him to come home. No man had ever made her feel that way before. Boredom could do strange things to a person, she supposed.

When he arrived home, she wanted to throw her arms around him, but stifled herself.

"Now that is a nice smile," he said, and flashed one in return.

How can a man be so awesome? she wondered, and stifled herself again. Instead, she said, "Have chocolate candy bars been invented?"

"A...yes. Do you have a hankering for one?"

"I changed my mind about the pies. I want to make and sell cookies. If I can get some chocolate bars then I can cut them up and put them in cookies."

"By cookies you must mean tea cakes."

"I think so."

"Huh. Candy bar in cookies. Is that not redundant?"

"I never looked at it that way," she said and chuckled. "Mark my words, you will love these cookies."

He poured some water from a pitcher into a large bowl and bent over to wash his face. She handed him more of a rag than a towel, but wished for a thick one like she had at home.

He laid the towel down and sat on his bedding. "What do you think about moving away from Cracker?"

"I don't know that I have any say in this, James." She shook her head with intensity. "I'm an interloper in your life."

"I understand what you are saying, but I want to make you a permanent part of my life."

"It's too soon to make that kind of decision. We just met...hardly know each other," she said.

"I believe I know you. You get to know a person when you see them at their lowest point."

"We...I've not seen you at your lowest point, so that is irrelevant to me."

His chin went up ever so slightly. "I have had my lowest point and do not wish to go there again."

She sighed and said, "Of course you don't. And I also don't want you to think what I've been through trumps your experiences. Heavens, no."

In two steps, Dixie stood in front of him and put a hand on his jaw in an effort to relax it. His dark eyes squinted down at her when she quietly said, "Okay, I stand by your decision of where to live, just let me know if and when you want to leave and I'll...I'll pack."

James took in Dixie's beautiful smile, her perfect teeth and full lips and started to sweat. Not from the heat, but from being in the same room for more than a moment.

Of course, she would follow him to the ends of the earth, she had no choice. So, he had to make proper decisions for her. Even though a woman today expected their husband to lead them, Dixie, as an adult, had not experienced this before.

Certainly a man made plans based on his family and their needs, decision-making new to him to boot. Accordingly, Dixie did not belong in this town.

He stood and Dixie's finger tips glided across his chin, tracing the stubble there. As he took a hold of her hand, someone pounded on the door.

"The stove is here, Mr. Brogan!" he heard through the diminutive cracks at the sides of the unfinished window, reminding him of another reason they needed to leave Cracker.

Dixie jumped up and down. "The stove! Now I can bake cookies." But when she saw it she lost her enthusiasm, but forced a smile for James. The baking trial and error would be difficult without someone to guide her.

Men congregated to help James plumb the stove pipe and then set it out through the back wall.

"Do you know much about baking, James?" she asked when the men left.

"I tend to be a stove top cook."

This new sight and then having to depend upon someone to help her get started, deeply frustrated her. The thought of putting too much change upon James made her want to go back to search for the cave she'd arrived in. Hard pressed to know how to accomplish this without James missing work frustrated her.

James turned toward her and she tried not to sound desperate when she said, "When will you be going out to look for gold again?"

"I do not know if I will be. I have orders left to fill and then my extra time should be spent making this cabin salable. I believe I must make a date to have everything completed so we can go. We cannot be here for the snow."

"Even though I know where the gold is?" she asked as simply as she could.

"There are things in life far more valuable than gold," he said with finality and she knew then that he was ready to move in a direction he had not planned to go until he'd met her.

"You look panicked, Dixie. What is wrong?"

A hundred thoughts seemed to flood through her mind, among them a ride on Morgan through the woods to look for the cave. If, as last time, her mission failed, she could be kidnapped, raped and killed. Obviously, James didn't want her to go and her logical mind wouldn't ask just anyone out here to help her or attempt the journey alone.

"Dixie?" He took her hand. "What is wrong," he said in words hardly heard.

James didn't deserve to have his horse stolen or a woman killed on his watch. In her circumstances, she had to be kind plus truthful.

She sat down and leaned against the wall of the cabin. "I've lost a lot, and you've been nothing but understanding." She wondered at what point he'd lose patience with her, and sincerely did not want this to happen. Still, she said, "Have you ever thought about what my century is like?" Before he answered, she shot in, "The comforts, the technology, and the medial advances are amazing. Did you know that you can get a horrible headache and take one or two pills and your headache will be completely gone? Did you know that you can ask an object what the weather report is and it will answer you in a human voice?"

"I bet it still gets the weather wrong," he answered, rather tongue-in-cheek.

She pretended to ignore him. "You can have a heart attack and survive with surgery."

His eyebrows furrowed. "How long do people live?"

"It is not unusual to see someone live into their nineties and some one-hundred."

"Huh," he simply said.

"The plumbing is all indoors. Flushable toilets."

"Huh."

"James, will you go back to my time with me? You and Morgan would be the only thing I'd miss."

"I will not have a car, money, a job, or an actual identity."

"But *I* have those things, James. I could help you get started."

"It flatters me that you want to take me with you, but I have watched you try to get started and I cannot wish that on anyone. If I have you here there is nothing I want in your time."

That had to be the sweetest thing she'd ever heard and she wanted to fling herself into his arms, but he backed away.

"You cannot make decisions when you are upset, Dixie. I am sorry that the oven brought up challenges you have never had to face, but you are a strong woman and you will survive."

He was right, except for the part about being strong, because she didn't feel strong most of the time these days. She had to carry on at least for the moment, and for more intent than purpose she turned, nodded and said, "Let's nail in a few more boards, James."

Cranston stood by the Brogan cabin and listened to the nailing. Now that her oven was delivered and put in, Mrs. Brogan couldn't want for much more.

Now she will keep warm, bake bread and cook to her heart's content while he prepared for winter by finding acorns so he could leach acid from them, enough to tan the hides of animals to wear among six feet of snow.

He had arrived about the same time as Mrs. Brogan. Somehow he didn't have even a tenth of her luck. There were no berries, fruits or nuts in season yet, so while she searched for a suitable mate, he ate grass and dandelions until he heard that men could chew on clovers, chickweed and cattail without dying. With his pocket knife, he tried not to kill a tree by taking only a marginal area of the bark to eat the inner side. He officially became un-human.

While she laughed and made eyes at Brogan, he wondered if he'd survive the winter. How could life be so unfair, he asked himself for the hundreth time. She was nothing, while at one time he had everything he ever wanted, including respect.

Perhaps a sick or malicious thought, but he wanted her to suffer for this injustice.

Chapter 13

The next day, Dixie continued working on the cabin following a repeating, wood overlaying pattern that James had trained her to do. When she'd gone as far as she could without him, she looked at the progress and smiled. She'd learned that doing something with your hands had its rewards. This building she'd helped to build would stand for some time to come, and a bit of her felt sorry she had to leave it.

She'd been ignoring the stove, basically mad at it for not being user friendly. After forcing herself to look at it, she decided that if she could learn a complex computer system, then she could certainly figure out a wood stove.

James had ordered the stove in preparation for the cool fall in the mountains, so he hadn't started it yet. Dixie opened each of the stove doors to study the layout of the cast iron oven. It stood on four artistically designed, club legs. The top had four circles you could lift off with a handle. Below she discovered a fire box along one side of an oven. She took a closer look at the adjustable dampers that obviously sent smoke up the chimney pipe. By looking closely and altering them, she realized she could control where the heat and smoke would go around the whole system and a way to heat the oven. And most likely the whole cabin and down the street.

Not wanting to burn the cabin down in ignorance, she sat and considered what to do next. She saw James's Bible and picked it up.

By the dog-eared edges of several pages, she could tell the book had been read widely. While flipping through, she didn't find any markings, which surprised her somehow. She decided that if the book was important to James, then she should start reading it likewise. Not for the first time did she wonder why she'd traveled in time and why it happened in particular to her. Perhaps here she could find a thought as to what her life may mean in the scheme of things.

The Christian faith took favor in the New Testament so she started reading about the birth of Jesus in Matthew.

***

Every time Dixie left the cabin, she had a bodyguard with her. Well, that's what it felt like anyway. James became her guide and teacher. Even though he probably had other things he could do, or simply rest, she enjoyed his company.

Many of the townspeople had missing teeth, dirty clothes and dirt on their extremities. Too late, she appreciated the dental care she got in her era, which was now the future. Yet many of the men in Cracker were here on a mission to find gold and return to their families. Cleanliness had a position further down on their priority list, and she couldn't blame them for staying dirty when they had a physically hard and dirty job.

***

Dixie pulled two loaves of bread from the oven just before James made it home. She turned to say hello and took plates from a shelf they had positioned on the wall of the cabin.

"Bacon and eggs. Smells good," he said, and turned to wash his hands in the basin.

"Sometimes we have breakfast for dinner in the future," she said.

He winked. "Yes, of course you do."

She spread some butter on slices of bread. "I want to make my own butter, this stuff is only slightly passable."

"Your arms are getting strong enough, I suppose, with all the hammering you are doing on the cabin."

"Yes, a silver-lining, I suppose."

"We will pack up next week after I post a notice of sale at the store."

When he continued to stare at her, Dixie lowered her eyes and said, "Sounds good." She knew he wanted an answer to his proposal, yet trying to be very patient as she stalled. It probably killed him.

"I decided to go back to Oregon City. I have family there and you may have a better chance of gaining employment if you so choose."

"Really?" she asked, intrigued.

James gave her a poker face, so she couldn't read him. But she knew he wanted her to continue to lean on him. She grew to want the marriage, too, but still wanted to be sure of it.

"I met Cranston," he said at length.

"Oh?"

"Yes, he stopped by to talk to Stephen, but he was not in."

"Huh."

"Seems he found some gold where you said it would be."

"I knew it! Did he tell you precisely where?"

"He seemed surprised when I told him you thought gold was there, too. But, no, he did not say exactly where, because the someone could come and take his gold."

"Makes sense."

She placed the food on his plate and handed it to him.

"This is good. You have come a long way in a short time, Dixie. You should be proud."

Dixie realized she did feel proud, even if this was not a headlining breakthrough news report in the newspaper. "Thank you. I am proud about being able to help build a cabin. I didn't even realize this could be something I liked to do."

"To realize your strengths is good."

"Yes, it is," she said, her chest welling with a sense of satisfaction.

James finished his meal and stood to place his plate and utensils in the wash basin. He turned and said, "I have enough money in a bank in Oregon City to more than get us started in a new life."

This, the first time he'd mentioned money, took her by surprise. Dixie hadn't been sure he had any money, but considered it his business until she made a commitment to him. Still, it didn't matter to her because he had the strong work ethic to do what needed to be done to provide for himself or a family. She could imagine him stopping anywhere and asking for work.

"You have no reply?" he asked.

"If you think you're making yourself more valuable to me, then you're wrong. Even without a penny, you are priceless, James."

Dixie could see emotion welling in his eyes and wanted to kiss him and more. Instead, she also moved to put her dishes in the wash pile. "I have diamonds you know," she said, looking up smiling.

"They are a precious memory of your parents and they will look very nice in your ears."

James touched her shoulder on his way out to tend to Morgan.

***

Cranston thought about the carefully planned meeting he had with Brogan. When he introduced himself as the neighbor who gave Mrs. Brogan supplies for the cabin, Brogan gave him a critical once over.

He waited for a thank you, but none came. Not that his wife hadn't already thanked him, still he expected a respectful note of gratitude.

Their "meeting" proved eventful as Brogan asked if he'd seen a cave while searching for gold. Instantly, he'd told Brogan no, but planned to use this bit of information to get closer to Mrs. Brogan. Like a lamb to the slaughter, she'd come with him, without a clue to his plan. Brogan had no idea he helped him, which delighted him to no end.

***

Dixie wondered about Oregon City, currently the largest city in Oregon. There had to be more jobs for women and a respectable room to rent. She imagined her diamonds could provide for a time, until she could find employment. Perhaps she could even get a job at a newspaper. She'd be willing to clean the place until she could get the ear of the office manager. Sadly, her word was all she had without a resume or proof of past work to present.

She knew, because of James's strong beliefs, he would require an answer to his proposal on this trip. He'd not lie to his family about their relationship and could probably find a family member to take her in if she declined marriage. Even though that wasn't a bad proposition, she didn't want to live with someone not of her own choosing.

It took one day to sell the cabin and half the contents. James bought another Morgan horse, scheduled to arrive at the blacksmith's shop sometime today. Tomorrow, they'd rise early, pack the horse and begin the long journey to James's hometown.

With James gone to finish up at work, she picked up the Bible again and perused it. At length, in Ephesians two, she read, "For by grace you have been saved through faith, and that not of yourselves; it is the gift of God."

She wrote down the verse and set the paper on the Bible. She needed to remind James of this verse, so that he would see that because of the cross he didn't have to earn his way back into heaven.

A knock on the door brought Dixie to one of the newly installed windows. Cranston stood, this time without gifts. Remembering James's word of caution she spoke through the door. "What do you want?"

"I have been a talkin' to your husband. Since you are movin', I asked him about where I should search for gold and he sent me here to confirm his thoughts with you."

She thought for a moment and then opened the door ever so slightly. "It's where you have been looking."

"Good day, Mrs. Brogan. I hear you are gettin' ready to move on to Oregon City."

"Yes. That's right."

After moments of rolling the brim of his hat, he said, "My golden luck is runnin' out and I wonder if you could rightly show me where I can find more."

"I haven't exactly seen it, so I have nothing to tell you. Good day, Mr. Cranston." She attempted to shut the door, but his foot intercepted.

"Can you at least tell me which side of the cave it is on?" he asked, his voice rising.

"You found a cave?" she asked, her heart starting to pound with excitement.

"Yes."

Dixie opened the door.

"Yes," he repeated and pointed in the right direction. "You seem to be interested in the cave. Does that mean I am right? My hopes are arisin'."

"Yes. Can you tell me more about this cave? Can you stand up in it?"

He nodded, swiftly. "I would be happy to show it to you. As you know, I am vera interested in findin' that gold."

"Can you wait a moment? I need to change my clothes."

"Certainly, ma'am. I am at your mercy," he said and bowed.

Her hands shook as she put the diamonds in a pocket of her jeans. She pulled them on, along with her top, and then nearly slid into her shoes. Finally, she had a way to get home, something impossible until now.

A little voice in Dixie's head cautioned her. Ignoring it, she flew out the door and started walking down the road with Cranston.

"Do you have family somewhere?" she asked.

"Yes, in Southwest Idaho."

"Oh? I'm surprised you're not searching for gold in Idaho, Idaho City in particular."

He waved a hand in dismissal. "It is a long story."

In quiet, they moved along the trail she and James had used to search for the cave. Simply confirmation, she believed.

The light green of spring had turned with the summer heat, leaving the grass of the pine forests yellow. The trails that had puddles dried into a lumpy uneven walkway from domestic or wild animal prints.

As she considered going back home, a joy such as she'd never experienced, filled her soul.

"Have you been inside the cave?" she asked.

"Yes. And like I said, it is tall enough to walk in."

"James and I looked for it, but couldn't find it."

"Did you tell anyone about the cave, other than your husband?"

He feared someone would get to the gold before him, she knew, and decided to calm his nerves.

"No, he's the only one, and I'm not certain he even believes there is one out here."

"Why are you leavin' if you can find gold? Most would want to find it?" he asked, with furrowed brow.

"He says Cracker is no place for a woman."

"He is right 'bout that." He looked at her through narrow eyes, then said, "I am surprised he brought you here."

Dixie only nodded, as she had no desire to tell him their story. Nearing their destination, she stopped mid-step and considered her plan to leave with James in the morning. Now, she wouldn't be moving after all and James had the freedom to stay in Cracker.

A cloud overhead covered the sun and her spirits dipped with the shadow that covered them. She tried to tell herself going home was what she really wanted and visualized her apartment, job, electricity and flushing toilet.

Still, her gut tightened and an emotional pang hit her chest. *James*, she thought, as if whispering to him in her mind. In her excitement and hurry, she didn't have the decency to write him a note, or more respectful, to say good-bye in person.

With each step her heart hurt more, making her realize she loved James more than she knew. She'd decided James could never really want to saddle himself with a conditioned, liberated woman such as herself, when a more malleable woman of this era made for a better fit. Still, it became clear now that everything he did for her was out of love, when she stupidly believed he only wanted her as a form of repentance. *Am I not worthy of his love?* she asked herself for the first time since she'd met James.

Looking ahead, Dixie focused on steadying her emotions. Her steps slowed, labored by heavy breathing, while his firm steps quickened. Now, closer to the cave, Cranston's face hardened.

What? She'd done nothing to offend him and struggled fiercely with the desire to turn back. Certainly they could come later, along with James.

Cranston had reached the area that Dixie had been through before. With hands on hips, he did a quick, hard search of his surroundings and then at her.

The more she moved toward him the more determined he became, telling himself she only amounted to an annoying insect he couldn't tolerate anymore. He had to think of her that way, because he came to Cracker with nothing and learned what it felt like to struggle for a teaspoon of decent food. Unlike Dixie who found the best looking guy in town to take care of her, charming him to take her out of here. Away to bigger and better things only she could determine. Unbelievable riches stacked up in the mind of someone who deserved nothing.

Well, he also had plans and they included extinguishing the life of this parasite. In the long run, he'd be doing Brogan a favor, too.

Cranston knew fear kept Dixie from coming further. "Where's the cave?" she asked in a firm, loud voice.

"Come closer, I'll show you."

Chapter 14

"No, I don't think so. I think I'll just wait here for awhile; catch my breath," said Dixie with hands on her knees for emphasis.

Cranston sighed long and hard. "No. Come *here*. We'll walk together to the cave. It's just over the rise."

No, she'd searched every inch, indentation or rabbit hole over the rise, and the cave wasn't there. She stepped backwards. "What do you know about the cave?"

"Everything you do. I've traveled here, too, and as far as I can tell, you are the only other person who has done the same."

"What is your real name?" she asked, suddenly realizing what may have happened.

"Ernie Welch."

Dixie recognized the name, but wondered why he would sneer as he said it. "I've decided I don't want to see the cave," she said, and wondered why no one else was in sight when she usually saw a man at every turn.

"I saw you washing clothes down at the creek. Don't you miss washing machines? And dishwashers, television, the computer and internet access?"

Not to mention cars, she thought.

"Don't you miss your family?" he continued, moving a hand for emphasis.

Of course she did, but she realized something important on her way out here, that she couldn't leave

James, that she'd probably dry up and blow away without him.

Instead of answering, she scanned the area for something to hit him with, because she had no doubt she'd have the opportunity to do so.

"What is it about me that scares you, Welch?"

"You don't scare me," he spit out. "I've been watching you two and I didn't like what I saw. I just don't want you around when I find more gold, then start changing history. Think of the things I can invent, or help invent. This is my era, my day to make it big."

"Beyond an introduction, you don't even know me. I haven't done anything to you to make you want to harm me," she finally said.

"*Come on.* You've looked down your nose at me, like at a wretched disease you didn't want to catch. I'm surprised you even followed me out here when moving on with Brogan fit your needs far better. Neither of you will ever have a moment for a hungry, destitute, homeless man like myself."

"Tell me this then, if you were hungry, destitute, and homeless, why didn't you reach out to me. Why not be honest and tell me you came through the cave into another time?"

"Ha! I do not run in your circles."

"We are not in high school, Ernie."

"Might as well be, and envious students like me, crazy if as you say, shoot the people who turn up their noses at them. Let me tell you something. I own the cave and these acres around it *and* the impressive gold nugget, but still I stand here with nothing."

Perhaps, she thought, that if she could keep him talking someone would come by and intervene. "That must be hard, I know it is difficult to lose everything you had. And of course you are not crazy, that's just a saying. And who would want to envy me and James? Come on, we can work this out somehow. You and I have more in common than anyone else. Think of the problems in the world that we can ward off together."

"Don't try to placate me," he said in a low voice and pointed his thumb at his chest. "You are my biggest problem and I plan to take care of you *and* your husband."

Dixie noted his words and in her ever-rising fear, she felt winded again.

She'd often wondered why she was sent to this time and never could name anything concrete. Yet, James was a fair trade for anything ever invented. She lost her parents, and that pained her dearly, but...everything in her would not let her move forward. Her emotions pulled her down like the figure of an old humpback woman. Yet, she couldn't stay this way, she had to fight for a life with James.

Dixie tried to bring forth memories of the action shows she'd seen on television, and every fighting woman trying to stay alive. Again she looked toward the ground for an object to hurl.

When Cranston took his first step toward her she turned and ran. Apparently, he had filled with adrenaline enforcing speed and power. Her days of jogging and body building exercise had dwindled to walking and stretching before taking the laundry down to the creek, and her legs felt the difference.

After grabbing her, he knocked her off her feet and the ground hit the side of her face so hard that she saw black spots. As he bent over her, the heel of his hand jabbed her nose and blood spurted out. In a split second before he hit her again, she pushed her foot hard between his legs. He doubled over while she took to her feet.

Her course took her to her original trail toward the water. As she'd believed then, water could take her toward others, especially to those panning for gold.

Oddly enough, as if a holiday, the forest had a quiet, eerie air to it that she'd never heard or experienced before.

***

James finished the job, cleaned out his work space and thanked Stephen for the opportunity to do business with him.

He had a lilt to his step as he walked back to the cabin, now ready to leave Cracker in hopes of establishing a more permanent life and a family with Dixie.

Love shown in Dixie's eyes, whether she realized it or not, and it would only be a matter of time before she succumbed to his proposal. A life in Oregon City, a far cry from the savage Cracker, had everything a woman could desire, including fellowship with other women. Dixie would no longer have to struggle on her own.

In fact, he was so happy that he flung open the cabin door ready to hug Dixie. His happiness dissipated after viewing the empty room. With a pounding heart, he moved toward the note on the Bible. It had a scripture about grace on it, but not a clue to her whereabouts.

Stephen was the only one in Cracker he trusted to spend time with Dixie alone, and he continued his work in the blacksmith shop. He searched his mind for anyone she might know besides the general store owner, and remembered Cranston.

When he found Cranston's tent, he opened the flap and stepped inside. Besides the usual garb of a man tent-living, he found several notes. One mentioned a Thomas Edison, Alexander Bell, the light bulb, toilet paper, windmills and pens. James did not know these men or of what the notes could mean. Nothing here pointed him to what could have happened to Dixie.

The only thing that would tie the two was that he sought for gold in the area that Dixie alluded to. Yet, the area had one other thing of importance to her. It saddened him deeply that she would go off to find the cave without saying anything.

Not saying good-bye was not like Dixie and it appeared she had only taken the clothes on her back, so he doubted she left on her own accord.

James came back to the cabin for Morgan and his gun. Never had he been so terrified and to steady himself he considered the scripture that Dixie wrote on the scrap of paper.

Morgan moved quickly, certainly sensing his concern. Dixie had been right to name the horse that was as much a part of the household as he was. She had softened his hard heart in many ways and he had to have this woman back or he would revert into a shell of a man.

"By grace you are saved," he said the verse aloud. He had heard it many times in the past. "By grace...you are saved."

Halfway there, he realized her intent. She still thought he wanted to marry her because he needed to serve others to be saved on judgment day. Perhaps he did at the beginning, he knew of no other way to come to terms with his past, but love for Dixie quickly tore away any other reason for wanting her. Still, it warmed his heart that she wanted to help him be right with God. If for no other reason, he had to find her to explain this to her.

James pleaded for God's grace again, to find Dixie unharmed.

***

Out of nowhere, two young Native American men stepped out into the clearing and having watched a million old westerns, Dixie didn't know which way to turn, which evil more prevalent. In a nanosecond, she realized that only one of them had plans to kill her, so she moved toward the feather-clad men.

When she glanced down to maneuver across a rocky path, an arrow whizzed by her ear. A garbled cry, and a thud, sounded behind her, but she still kept running in the event her number was next. She circled around to the area in which she came, because it was the crosscut to town.

Even though the 1870s proved to be more hellish for her than the future, she continued to run from the cave to James and a future with him.

As if she'd conjured him up, he appeared up the trail on Morgan. Morgan picked up his step when he saw her in the distance. Somehow, the sweetness of it made her cry.

Nearing them, she started to worry about the Native Americans behind her and what they might do to James. He looked beyond her and straightened in his saddle and she knew he'd seen them.

His hand went to his side and she shook her head, then stumbled from not watching her way. He didn't miss her cue and put both hands on the reigns.

At Morgan's side, James pulled her up behind him. He handed her a white handkerchief he took from his pocket, and she wiped the blood from her nose and head. Only then did she focus and look at what she'd missed behind her.

Still, James moved toward the two men as casual as if he wanted to comment about the weather. In a moment, she realized that this was not his first rodeo.

"They saved me from Cranston," Dixie said, and stared at him lying on the ground with an arrow in his chest, somehow surprised that he didn't disappear into the future.

He put a hand on her leg to silence her. Behind James her fears subsided somewhat, because he knew enough not to run, like he tried to do the right thing at the moment.

Dixie could feel the core of him, his countenance changing into the soldier he once was and even with her life at stake her soul wanted to cry out at the hardship of anyone having to fight others in such a brutal way. She hated that she put him in this position.

James stopped Morgan about twenty feet in front of the men. Two firm foreign words came out of James's mouth, repeatedly. After what seemed like hours, one answered with a head nod.

They looked at each other, to James and then crooked their heads so they could see Dixie. One pointed behind him with a thumb, obviously to Cranston, and then mimed a fist punch to the face, then jogging and an exaggerated, frightened face. The other man pointed back at her and touched his chest before mimicking shooting an arrow at Cranston's heart.

James nodded. A word was said by one, along with a motion connecting Dixie to James and he nodded again. The man moved toward them and with a few grunts and arm swings he made notice of her pants and shirt, then finished with fingers making stripes down his head. If she wasn't so petrified she'd laugh at his allusion to her dress and hair weave being out of the norm of things.

"Home," James said and used his hands to represent a dress.

The men climbed back onto their horses, moved past them and pointed in the distance. "Reservation," she heard one say. He didn't look too happy about it either.

"Living a bit of history," she said to James. "It is amazing to have conversed with Native Americans."

"Native American's?" he asked.

"Yes, Indians are called Native American's in the future."

"I suppose they were here first."

Her whole body started shaking. "They saved my life," she said with a sob.

Morgan stood still while James took her hands and pulled her arms around him. "I am glad you are safe."

That's all he said, no chastisement or finger pointing.

***

James waited for Dixie to explain what happened, because he did not want to put false notions in his mind, to fuss over hurt feelings that did not belong.

"I'm not usually one to act without thinking, but I did that today. Cranston came to the cabin and asked about the gold. He told me that you said it was okay for me to go with him to find it. I know now that you wouldn't have sent me anywhere without you, but when he mentioned the cave, I followed him out here."

He wished she understood him better. "No, I would not have sent you."

"I'm *so* sorry."

"I understand that you want to go back to your time," he said, hoping to hide his sadness.

"But that's just it. The closer I got to the cave, which is still buried by-the-way, the more I realized that I didn't want to go. Sometimes I tell myself that it would be better for both of us if I went back."

He shook his head. "It would not be better for me, Dixie."

James could only see her side view but he could see sadness there, followed by a tear. "I understood what you meant by the Bible verse you left at the cabin. I cannot be saved by works, but by grace given to me by the Son of God."

She nodded and sniffed.

Morgan shifted his weight and James knew he should move on. Still, he said, "I had forgotten, so thanks for helping me with that."

"I know you've been through a lot. And now, instead of running, you stopped to talk with the Native Americans. You're a good man."

He smiled. It was hard to get used to the new name, yet it suited them well. "They are not all bad people. They have lost more than I can imagine."

"They saved me from death. Thankfully, they saw what was going on."

"I do not understand why Cranston wanted to hurt you."

Her face hardened. "He told me his name is Ernie Welch and then I realized he came through the cave as well. He is the man I came out here to interview for the newspaper, who owned the property, and the gold nugget. He came through the tunnel with even less than I had, yet, he didn't approach me about needing anything. He watched us and envied us, even though we could have helped him, James. He had plans to find more gold then become a notable and rich man, by knowing what and who made inventions in the future. Even though he couldn't make friends with us, he planned to make friends with the innovators before moving in on their territory.

"Cranston, er…Welch, didn't want me to flourish. His struggling to survive here in Cracker, plus his trumped up envy of us, seemed to break him."

"Envy has ruined a man many a time," added James. "Fear and loss can destroy him, too. The man did not appear healthy, all but skin and bones."

She nodded. "Why are some people more blessed than others?"

"Since the war, I have thought about this very issue. Why did I live while many died? Some things we will never know for sure, but I think we all have something to be thankful for, no matter how small. If you are thinking about your journey as compared to Welch's, you are two people with different experiences from birth to this day. He seemed to understand early on what his circumstances were, yet he didn't seek help outside of what he could do himself. He did not appear to have any hope within or without."

"Yeah. I had my diamond earrings to sell and begin again and someone that looked out for my welfare. He had nothing."

"If we had known we could have helped him here in Cracker, or he could have gone to Sumpter and found a church for a helping hand. Basically, he chose to go it alone and could not withstand the turmoil. What he did manage to do was minimize others, to place himself in a higher more deserving place."

Dixie nodded and then sighed.

"You are a strong woman. You want to be useful, earn your own way, wanted to pay me back any way you could. You always had hope and learned to look to God for help with your circumstances. The most important lesson I have learned in life is that whatever happens to me, God will be there with me, no matter what happens. All you really can control is how you react to what happens to you."

James took a deep breath, before he spoke again, "You have to be disappointed, not finding the cave."

"No, along the long walk I realized I didn't want to leave you. Not ever. Whatever the future holds for me, I will trust in God. Whether I have to wash clothes at the creek or tend to twelve babies, or have a job outside the home, it doesn't matter because we'll go there together, my good man."

He pulled her head to his chest and held it there until Morgan shifted his weight again. "Stephen and I will come back and bury him on his property. Then we will finish packing," he said, and cleared his voice.

***

Dixie knew the long trek would be hard, but there wasn't anyone in any century she'd like to travel with more than James. On the way to Sumpter, she debated about a name for the second Morgan horse.

"How about Gulliver, Flicka, or Black Beauty?" she asked.

"A…no."

"Mr. Ed, Hidalgo, Shadowfax, or Pilgrim?" she asked with a chuckle.

His eyebrows furrowed. "Mr. Ed? And who would name their horse Shadowfax?"

"I'm naming horses from fiction books over the years."

After a moment of silence, he said, "I think Grace is a good name for her.

"Oh, that's perfect."

In Sumpter they stopped to get married. She straightened her muscles and her skirt upon arrival and put a shaking hand through her hair. She glanced at James and wondered if he was nervous, too.

"We need to go pick out a ring first," he said.

Despite her nervousness her heart sung at the idea of picking out a ring with the man she loved.

"You want a gold band or a diamond?"

Thinking of doing housework the old fashioned way, she said, "A gold band will be nice."

They found matching bands, which made her heart expand even further knowing he wanted to have a ring, too.

James reached deep into a pocket and came up with a gold nugget which he used to pay for the rings.

Dixie had been thinking on the way to town that she wanted to have their picture taken. After the simple ceremony they had lunch and left the area. The photo, after processing, would arrive later in Oregon City.

After they'd gone a distance, Dixie turned back to say good-bye to the area that brought her so much loss, yet so much gain, but would never see again.

Epilogue

People of the 1800s knew that exercise was a part of their existence, not a set time to work out. The idea of fancy workout clothes now seemed silly to someone who had to replace their shoes three times on the partial walk west. Still, Dixie had never been in better shape and it only cost her time.

Closer to Oregon City, James wired his family and a party of friends and relatives met them to celebrate their return and marriage. Certainly, she wished she'd had a bath and wore a nice dress, but the family greeted her warmly anyway. Not a critical eye was to be seen. So glad their James made it home, no one even seemed to notice her auburn weave.

Even though she'd lived primitively in Cracker, in Oregon City she'd dwell in a more civilized manner, perhaps not as elegantly as James's father's home, but as an attorney James would have what they needed and probably more.

The smell of a magnificent spread of food lured them in, amazing Dixie with more choices than she'd had in a couple of centuries. Someone here could help her figure out this way of cooking and she looked forward to female advice and bonding.

So thankful to fill her plate with such delectable food, she said a silent prayer of thanks and then caught James's eye and smiled as they were home at last.

Present Day in the Twenty-first Century

Crawford Stone took a nervous breath before knocking on the apartment door, gripping the last request of his belated best friend, Travis Benson.

While he waited for a reply, he considered the sealed manila envelope addressed to a Dixie Lea of Boise, Idaho. Perhaps he should have read the contents and made sense of the visit, but his love for his friend wouldn't let him. He hoped that the envelope held something good for the person he could hear unlocking the door.

In the doorjamb stood an attractive, auburn-haired young woman of average weight and height.

"Yes?"

"A…my name is Crawford Stone. I have an envelope for you. Here. It's from my best friend's attorney. It appears Travis Benson wanted me to hand deliver this to you. I don't know what it is. Do you recognize the name?"

Dixie liked the looks of this man, Crawford, but suspicion ran rampant through her. After taking the envelope, she said, "Stand back please."

"Of course."

"I've never heard of this man." Still she ripped open the flap and looked inside. Another envelope was at the bottom and she pulled it out. The return address space on the white standard-sized envelope said Travis Benson, but no address listed. Sure enough, her name and address was listed as the recipient.

The envelope was well-worn as if it had been handled many times. The letter inside barely held together and the cursive writing faint.

"I hope it's something good," said Crawford. "Travis was a good guy."

"What happened to him?" she asked before reading.

"Policeman. Died on duty. Very sad to be cut down like that before thirty years old.

"Yes. I'm sorry for your loss," she said and nodded before returning to the letter. "Was your friend somewhat of a jokester?"

"He had a sense of humor, but jokester, no. What is it, what does it say?"

She wondered if she should read it aloud, before sending the man on his way. *Why not include him in on the joke*, she thought. Perhaps it could help with his grieving in some way.

"It is dated 1872, from Oregon City, Oregon. The letter inside is addressed to me, too." She continued to read the two page letter a moment before adding, "Seems another Dixie Lea time-traveled from our century, this year in fact, to somewhere between Cracker and Sumpter, Oregon."

"I don't even know where that is," said Crawford, with a frown.

"Neither do I." Dixie gave him a half smile, without humor. "She met and married Lieutenant Colonel James Brogan in Sumpter, Oregon. The printing is very similar to mine. This is ridiculous, wouldn't you say?"

"It is rather odd," he answered with a furrowed brow.

Revolted, she started to hand the letter and envelope back to Crawford, when something fell out. He bent to pick it up. "It looks like a picture of you with a man, but it's an old photo."

"Sure, let me see," she reached out, while tapping a foot with impatience.

The picture was indeed of her with a man, a handsome man of whom she wouldn't have forgotten. This was a recent photo of her, because of the recent feathering of hair around her face, or maybe even a doppelganger. "I don't remember this at all. I don't have these clothes."

"Perhaps it was taken at a fair or carnival, you know where you can dress up in old west clothes and have your picture taken."

"No, I would have remembered this. And I might add that I have nothing of real value besides some diamond earrings. So, I would be a poor choice if someone wanted to dupe me for my money."

He shook his head and cleared his throat before moving to another thought. "You know, Travis talked many times about time travel. I'd go over to his place and catch him studying books on the subject, or arguing with his sister over the plausibility. I just thought he was heavy into science fiction. I wished now I would have paid more attention. I'll have to think about this."

She nodded while studying the letter.

"Perhaps we could go to coffee?" he asked.

Dixie looked up from her letter and frowned.

"So we can talk about this letter, some more. Maybe I can read it and think back about what Travis had shared with me in the past.

Even though she doubted the honesty of the letter, she didn't think coffee out with a handsome man could cause any harm. Yet, she was not so stupid to go with him in his car. "Let me grab my bag. I'll meet you at the corner coffee shop," she said, pointing west.

Stay tuned for book two in the Gold Club series.

About the Author

Mary Vine is the author of contemporary romantic fiction books MAYA'S GOLD, A PLACE TO LAND, SNAKE RIVER RENDEZVOUS and historical novella WANTING MOORE, published by Black Lyon Publishing. Through Melland Publishing, LLC, she has published a romantic mystery, A HAUNTING IN TRILLIUM FALLS, a romantic time travel, A NUGGET OF TIME, and an inspirational children's book, THE BIG GUY UPSTAIRS. She has also published two children's books by author Velma Parker, EMMA COMES THROUGH and MOLLY'S MONKEYSHINES. Mary, and her husband can usually be found in Southwest Idaho or Northeast Oregon.